D0425512

CEDAR PARK PUBLIC LIBRARY
5 4161 00116411 5

the SPIRIT LINE

To Elaine Koster, for pointing us in the right direction, and to Regina Hayes, for showing so much faith in us

Chapter One

"GOOD MORNING, early risers. It's six A.M. and time for the Dawn Patrol. In national news, congressional hearings begin . . ."

Crystal Manyfeathers blindly tapped the off button on her clock radio. "Give me a break. . . ." She kicked back the blanket, then swung around as she sat up in bed, her feet touching the cool concrete floor.

"Why can't at least one station within a hundred miles start the day with music instead of news and weather?" she grumbled. While trying to get her eyes adjusted to daylight, Crystal reached up and untangled the tiny headphones from her waist-length ebony hair. Her cassette player was still under the pillow, and the AC adapter cord extended over to the wall where it was plugged in. She must have fallen asleep last night before her tape had stopped. She always liked the distraction of music when she went to bed. It kept her from thinking too much.

Crystal stood and stretched. Outside, on the east-facing front porch of the house, she could hear her father offering prayers to the dawn.

"How can you stand there and pray to the gods after what happened to Mom?" she muttered, then brushed away a tear before it spilled down her cheek. Her family had fallen apart. Her mom was gone forever, and no gods would ever change that. Crystal wrapped her arms around herself, trying to fend off the darkness that crept into her heart every morning after she woke up.

Forcing herself to get moving—today was Monday—Crystal briefly considered giving up her morning run to work at the loom. She felt closer to her mom when she was weaving than at any other time. Her mother had taught her all she knew about weaving—the special songs, what each tool represented, and all the techniques that made a Navajo rug special. But the work required precision and wasn't something she could rush through before going to school.

Determined to shake off the blues, Crystal slipped her long legs into baggy jogging pants and pulled her turquoise and gold Rock Ridge Golden

Eagles sweatshirt over her head, struggling to push her arms through the sleeves.

"Feels funny. . . . Oh, great—it's on backward." Crystal sat back down on the bed, suddenly realizing that she was talking to herself now—out loud. How long had *that* been going on?

Two minutes later she stood again, her running shoes laced up, firm, but not tight enough to cut off her circulation. Tiptoeing through the living room, Crystal peeked out the front door and saw her father heading to the corrals. Before her mom had died, Crystal had always helped him feed the animals, but now, things between them were just too strained. Instead of going out with him before breakfast every morning, she trained by running two miles across the mesa.

Crystal jogged up the dirt road, then cut to the right onto a well-worn path leading to the top of the boulder-encrusted mesa, the rich reds and browns glowing from Sun, still low in the clear, ice-blue sky. She kept an eye out for rattlesnakes all along the winding trail, knowing they sometimes curled up on flat rocks to bask in the warmth of Sun's rays.

The reservation here was beautiful. The scent of resin from the low, wide piñon and juniper trees, a familiar and oddly comforting aroma, enhanced the charm of the wind-sculpted pines surrounding her. But as she ran today, Crystal was focused on her most important goal—leaving the reservation as soon as she possibly could.

For the past fifteen years she'd lived in the middle of nowhere, suffocated by her father's traditional culture. As the rest of the world was running into the new millennium at full stride, they didn't even own a TV set, let alone a home computer. She could hardly wait until she graduated from high school so she could join the real world. Crystal knew she would miss the land, but moving on was something she'd made her mind up about already.

A half hour later, showered and dressed, she looked into the small mirror she'd talked her parents into buying. Crystal checked out her jeans and the gold, long-sleeved, nylon jersey she often wore. *What I wouldn't give for a hair dryer,* she thought. At least it was only mid-September, and not too cold outside, so she wouldn't have to towel dry her hair to death.

Crystal took a quick look around her room and pulled her top blanket up far enough to make it look like she'd at least tried to make the bed. Finished for now, she walked into the kitchen and turned on the small radio resting on the countertop.

After changing the station to one that played country-western music, she put on the coffee and scrambled six eggs with a half cup of green chile. When the eggs were done, she stuffed the mixture into flour tortillas and rolled them up, making breakfast burritos.

Hearing footsteps on the porch, she quickly placed four of the burritos on a plate for her father and put the other two on a plate for herself. Last of all, she poured coffee into two mugs.

"Good morning, daughter." Her father's gravelly voice came out clear and strong above the sound of Brooks and Dunn as he walked into the kitchen.

Her father picked up his plate of burritos from the counter, paused to switch the radio station to the local news as usual, then sat down.

"Tastes weak," he said after taking a cautious sip of coffee.

"We were nearly out. I forgot to tell you we were running low. I guess I should have just made one cup instead of two." Crystal took a sip from her own mug, which was half coffee and half milk.

As usual, they both ate without speaking. Crystal noted that her father hadn't even looked at her yet. It was a habit he'd picked up since her mom had died. Maybe it was because as everyone always said—

or more correctly used to say—Crystal looked like her mother. Although Navajos rarely spoke about anyone who'd recently died, her mom had been gone a year now. Sometimes Crystal couldn't help but wonder if her dad would have been happier alone than with her around to remind him of Mom. She knew she'd be happier away from all the reminders.

Crystal finished her coffee and her first burrito, then decided she didn't want the second one. "I'll save this for your lunch," she mumbled, getting up and tracking down a piece of aluminum foil the right size from a drawer. They reused the clean pieces to save money.

Crystal returned to the bedroom and reached past her cross-country running trophies and blue ribbons to get the yellow legal pad she used for taking notes during U.S. history. Stuffing it and her math book into her pack, she walked to the kitchen. Her father was standing by the table, listening to the weather report. "There's some money," he said, gesturing toward the table. "Try to pick up coffee on the way home from school. I'll be south of Bad Water today with the herd."

He turned off the radio, grabbed his worn, sweat-stained straw hat and leather gloves from the table, then walked out the back door.

Crystal picked up the three dollar bills he'd left

for her and put them in her pocket. Taking the long, graceful strides that had made her a cross-country champion in the Four Corners region, Crystal headed down the dirt track. She heard the sound of a gate closing and turned her head in time to see her father carrying his saddle out of the tack room. Howdie, his big gelding, was already haltered and tied up at the hitching rail.

"Bye, Dad!" Crystal yelled.

Her father looked at her for the first time today, nodded, then turned back to Howdie.

Why did I bother? Crystal thought. *He's already used all his words for the week talking about the coffee.*

Twenty minutes later, Crystal stepped up onto the porch of the Hudson Trading Company, a fancy name for the cozy, corrugated-roof adobe building beside a steep terra-cotta-tinted sandstone cliff. The trading post was run by Mr. Albert, the Anglo trader. Navajos always called white people Anglos, although by and large, most weren't from Northern Europe or wherever Anglo-Saxons came from.

"Hey, Birdie, right on time again," Henry Tallman called. He was leaning against one of the posts on the wooden porch—his usual position in the mornings.

"Hi, Junior." Crystal waved. Almost everyone around here called Henry by his nickname, a common habit among Navajos, who believed real names had power and shouldn't be used casually.

She herself actually preferred being called Crystal, but ever since Junior had made his decision two years ago to follow in his father's footsteps and become a *hataalii,* a Navajo medicine man, he'd begun calling her Birdie, a joke based on her last name—Manyfeathers.

These past few months, as Junior's apprenticeship had intensified, he'd become much more attuned to the Navajo culture. He'd even started carrying a *jish* at his belt—a medicine pouch filled with substances that would protect the wearer.

"You look half asleep," she said, poking him in the ribs gently.

He smiled through half-closed eyes. "You sure? I was trying for two-thirds."

"Maybe you should run with me before breakfast. Watching for snakes always helps get your eyes open." Crystal sat down on the porch, placing her backpack beside her and dangling her legs over the edge.

Junior eased down to join her, placing his own book bag behind hers. "I don't need exercise. I need to go to bed earlier. To be honest, I think I've been walking here in my sleep every morning. Half the time I don't even remember the trip."

"You're on automatic, that's what it is." Crystal felt sorry for him. Junior had been keeping late hours recently with Henry Senior, who was teaching him the songs, chants, and ceremonial steps necessary to become a Navajo *hataalii*. Junior would have to memorize every detail of the healing ceremonies perfectly. Traditionalists believed that even a single mistake by a healer during a Sing could cause the gods to ignore their efforts or, in some cases, make everything worse.

Of course she'd never been able to understand why Junior believed all that. It just didn't make sense for anyone their age to follow the old ways. "You can sleep on the bus later."

"Nobody can sleep on the bus, except maybe for Mr. Anderson," Junior said solemnly.

Crystal laughed. Mr. Anderson was their bus driver. He was also the school custodian and the father of her Anglo friend Holly.

Sitting together, Junior and she listened for the sound of the school bus that picked them up each morning and took them on a twenty-minute ride through the shady foothills of the Chuska Mountains.

There was no town of Rock Ridge—just the school and some teacher housing.

"How's that rug going, Birdie?"

"I really wish you'd call me Crystal," she said. "I know you're trying to follow the Way, but I don't believe in all that stuff. So what do you say I call you Junior and you call me Crystal?"

"I'm not trying to force anything on you. I just need to use the old ways, now that I'm studying to be a Singer, and that means no names." He gave her a long, thoughtful look, as if trying to figure something out.

"What?" She'd seen that look on Junior's face before, mostly when he thought she wasn't looking. He'd done that off and on for several months, making her wonder what he was thinking. It was almost as if he had a secret he wanted to share, but he hadn't quite made up his mind whether to let her in on it or not.

"Sometimes I just don't understand you," he said at last. "You say you don't care about Navajo tradition anymore, but you weave almost every day, and that's a traditional craft. And you're going to go through the *Kinaaldá* ceremony this weekend, right?"

"I weave so I can sell the rugs. I'll need that money so I can get off the rez after high school. The womanhood ceremony . . . well, that's for my dad, not me. I'm only doing it because he's made a big deal about it being the last thing I can do for my mom. I don't want to hurt him when I can give him what he wants just by jumping through a few hoops. I do still love him, even though we don't agree on much. But that doesn't mean I believe in all that traditional Navajo stuff."

"But you *are* Navajo," Junior repeated.

"Yes, but I'm myself, too."

"Your mom would never have understood—" He stopped speaking abruptly, aware of how much Crystal missed her mom. "Sorry," he muttered. "It's too early. My mouth isn't connected to my brain yet."

As Junior sat there in silence, pretending to be extremely interested in his shoes, Crystal's throat tightened so much it hurt.

"That's okay," she said after a moment. "Sometimes, when I first get up, I forget she's gone. I even go automatically to the living room to find her." Her mother had always said that there was strength and power in the time right before dawn, and those who slept through it missed the best part of the day. Her mother had loved everything about the old ways and had tried hard to teach her all about the strength and beauty of Navajo traditions. But her mom was gone now, and her Navajo beliefs hadn't saved her.

Now Crystal was determined to follow her own path. She'd use the craft her mother had taught her—the one thing she did better than anyone else—to make a new start for herself as far away from here as possible. Her mother wouldn't have approved, and knowing that made her sad, but Crystal's mind was made up.

Junior bent down to pick up a few pieces of gravel, then flipped one rock at a time with his thumb, trying to hit a pop bottle cap farther out on the empty parking lot. "Still hoping to get a track scholarship?" he asked.

"Sure. Even if my rugs end up selling for hundreds of dollars each, I can't weave fast enough to pay for four or more years of college."

"Yeah, I hear you. I hope to be able to go to college as well, before returning to the rez. But we have to make it through three more years of high school first," Junior responded, flipping his last pebble. This one hit the metal cap squarely, flipping it right side up. "Yes!"

Crystal looked over at him with raised eyebrows. "You've been doing that every morning since school started, and you never hit that bottle cap until you only have one pebble to go and the bus is in sight. But you always hit it then. Care to explain what's going on?"

"Coincidence? Magic? Just plain luck?" He smiled at her. "Maybe someday I'll tell you my secret of stone flipping." He grew still, then stood. "The bus is coming. Let's go."

"Where?" she asked, looking down the road and seeing nothing. A breath later she saw the rooster tail of dust kicking up behind the approaching yellow school bus. "You're messing with my mind again, Junior."

Chapter Two

"WHERE DO you want to sit?" Junior asked as soon as they were on the bus. As usual, it was empty except for the bus driver, Mr. Anderson.

"In our usual place." Crystal had learned from experience that the noisy kids sat in the back and the quiet ones toward the front. Those who wanted to be bounced around sat in the seats above the back tires. She and Junior usually ended up in the third seat back, on the opposite side from the driver, so the morning sun wouldn't be in their eyes.

"You never told me how the rug was going," Junior said as they brought out their math homework.

"I should finish weaving it today after school, or maybe tomorrow if I get a late start or have a problem with the weather. It's a real pain that the loom's too big to keep inside. The tarp protects it from rain and all, but I can't weave when the weather's bad, or after dark." She looked over at him and added, "You'll like this rug. You should come see it when you get a chance. I'm using a Chief's Blanket design. It's woven in blue, red, white, and black wool with wide and narrow stripes. I dyed the wool myself and I didn't take a shortcut by using commercial dyes. Blue was the toughest color, but I followed the way my mom taught me, boiling sumac and pulverized clay together." Crystal had a moment's panic when she couldn't find her math paper, but remembered she'd left it folded in her book. "Mr. Albert says he already has people who are interested in my rug."

"How's your dad feel about you selling your rugs? Does he know that you plan to use the money to move away?"

"We haven't talked about it."

"Why don't you just sit down and tell him what's going on?" Junior asked.

"I try but he's really hard to talk to since . . ." Crystal's voice started to break again, and she cleared her throat. "Let's get back to the homework. Do we have the same answers?"

"Except on number twelve. I have *y* equals nine point three, and you have nine point two seven five. I rounded my answer off, I guess," Junior said. "What did Mr. Price want us to do?"

"Let's see." She checked her assignment page. "It doesn't say to round off, but it doesn't say not to either."

"Let's give the answer both ways," Junior suggested.

"Okay." They both wrote the extra information. Then Crystal put her paper back into her backpack, which was on the seat beneath the window. Junior had kept his stuff between them ever since fourth grade, when some of the other kids on the bus had accused him of having a girlfriend.

"How's your history paper going? I showed Mr. Teeter my note cards yesterday, and he gave me an A plus. How did you do?" Junior asked.

"My topic is American Indian treaty violations, but he says I'm going to have trouble finding enough references. He recommended I try to get to the school library and check the Internet. He thought the Library of Congress site might have copies of the actual documents."

"You're probably the only one in class who could understand all that legal jargon. You think you'll find it on the Internet?"

"I'm not sure. I was planning to just get the information I needed from tribal Web sites, but he says I have to compare what the actual treaty says with what was done, before I draw any conclusions. He says he wants me to stay objective."

"Well, we still have two weeks before the papers are due. You'll work it out."

Crystal nodded, then noticed Junior had his eyes shut.

The bus finally pulled up by the concrete-block buildings nestled in a narrow canyon between two piñon pine–covered ridges. Here, the state provided public schooling from kindergarten through high school for this part of the rez. Crystal was the first one off, followed by Junior.

"See you in class," Crystal called out to him as a couple of her friends approached. Seeing Melvin Jolly coming up to join Junior, she waved at him. "Hi, Shorty."

Melvin, a short, stout kid with a buzz cut, waved back at her. "Hey, Crystal! Yo, J.R." Shorty faked a high five at Junior, who did the same, missing his friend's hand by a good foot.

"Later," Junior called to Crystal, then nodded at his pal. The two walked away already deep in conversation.

Crystal went to greet her friends, careful to avoid looking at Junior as he walked off. The last thing she wanted was for anyone to start labeling them as a couple. She and Junior were just friends, but lately they'd been spending a lot of time together. Since they were from different clans and not subject to Navajo taboos about dating "relatives," their friends were all tempted to assume a lot of things that just weren't true.

"Hi, Crystal. Did my dad rattle everyone's teeth again this morning?" Holly joked. Holly, a skinny, red-haired Anglo girl with pale skin and very ordinary looks, was popular at school, probably because she was so friendly. She also came from a large family and was just as poor as most of the Navajo students, so she wasn't stuck-up or patronizing either. Her mother was one of the elementary teachers.

Lucinda, Crystal's cousin, was the shortest tenth grader in school, but she ran as fast as a jackrabbit and was on the cross-country team with Crystal. "Junior sure gave Shorty a dirty look when he called you Crystal," Lucinda said.

"It bugs him because that makes it harder for him to remember not to use anyone's real name. Learning the old ways is hard."

Holly looked at both of them curiously. "Come again?"

"Navajo names are supposed to contain power, and using them too much burns up your energy, or something like that," Crystal explained to her Anglo friend, then turned to verify it with Lucinda.

"Close enough. But there are a lot of Navajos, especially the younger ones, who don't believe in all that stuff anymore," Lucinda added. "And the truth is that without using names, it's really hard to keep track of who's talking to whom, particularly at family gatherings." Lucinda elbowed Crystal. "Remember?"

Crystal laughed, then, seeing the expression on Holly's face and knowing she was feeling left out, hurried to explain. "Last spring, after a long ceremonial, a lot of our clan members were standing around waiting to be served dinner," she said. "One of my little cousins was making a pest out of himself running around yelling and screaming, but his mother just ignored him instead of making him sit down. Finally he stepped on his aunt's toe. She was in the marines and is as big and mean as they come. When she yelled, 'Sit down and shut up,' half of the people there sat down so fast they nearly fainted."

Lucinda nodded. "Crystal and I started laughing and soon everyone else was laughing so hard it took almost forever to stop."

"Was that ceremony anything like the womanhood ritual they're doing for you next weekend, Crystal?" Holly asked. "Or can you say?"

"I can. And no, the ceremony with my noisy cousin was something completely different. The *Kinaaldá* is to show us what's expected of a Navajo woman and to call down the blessings of the Holy People. Once I make it through that, I won't be looked on as a kid anymore. But it's grueling. It's like a test of endurance. You have to do all sorts of things—chores Navajo women have done for a century or more—but without resting."

"You mean like cooking and sewing and taking care of the animals?" Holly asked.

"It's much more complicated," Lucinda said, shaking her head sadly. "She's given three lambs and a goat, and has to convert them into a meal for fifty relatives, all cooked over an open fire—the animals, not the relatives," Lucinda said. "Then she cleans up everything, does the dishes, washes everyone's clothes, sews a blouse and skirt from scratch, shears twenty sheep, converts their wool into yarn, and uses it to weave a rug. After that she builds a hogan, a complete, traditional Navajo home with six log walls, a roof, and a blanket for a door. Then she memorizes a complete healing ceremony, and has to beat a horse in a five-mile foot race. And that's just on the first day," Lucinda explained in a somber tone. "It almost killed me last May when I went through it."

Holly's mouth dropped open. "No! You've got to be kidding!" She looked at Lucinda, then back at Crystal, who was shaking her head sadly.

Then Lucinda cracked a smile, and both Navajo girls began to laugh.

"I *knew* you were making it up. What do you really have to do, Crystal?" Holly's face was as red as her hair.

"Well, we're not supposed to tell non-Navajos everything about our ceremonies, but I'll have to cook a special cake over coals in a hole that's dug into the ground, memorize prayers, and do lots of running. It used to take four days, but now they've shortened it to two, so kids don't have to miss school. What makes it all even harder is that I won't be able to go to sleep. I'll have to stay awake all night while prayers are sung."

"You also won't be allowed to eat much, or drink a lot of water, or anything else that might make you fat and lazy as an adult. Then there's the molding, but that's fun. I'm kind of short, if you hadn't noticed, so one of the things they did to me was to pretend to stretch me out—to make me taller, you know?" Lucinda added.

"And, at the last, I'll have to race a bunch of boys, and beat them," Crystal said.

"That part shouldn't be too hard for you. You

run faster than most of the boys anyway. Will Junior be one of the boys running?" Holly asked.

"Sure. His dad will be the *hataalii* at the ceremony, so Junior will probably be there the whole time. But none of the boys will be wanting to beat me, since tradition says they'll get old first if they do."

"I bet Junior is still going to make you really run for a while. He likes you, Crystal," Holly said with a sly smile. "Everyone knows."

Just then, the bell rang. "Saved by the bell," Crystal said with a laugh, and they began to walk toward the building.

As Crystal stood in front of her locker gathering what she needed for her first class, she thought about her *Kinaaldá*. She'd go through it to please her dad, but that ceremony didn't have anything to do with *her* future. She wasn't going to end up herding goats, or hauling water, and struggling to get by in the winter when a heavy snow could strand a family at home for weeks.

She wanted skills she could use in the modern world, where making a life for yourself required talents the ancient ones could never even have imagined from these lonely mesas. As far as she was concerned, the culture of her ancestors was dead, and she was moving on. But even though the ceremony didn't mean much to her, she still intended to prepare so she'd do well at each of the tasks. She was doing this for her dad, and she was determined to make him proud of her that day.

Hearing the next bell, Crystal hurried down the hall. Her first class was math, and Mr. Price, an Anglo married to a Navajo woman, was easygoing and fair. She was making A's in his class, and was planning on taking algebra, then geometry, and lastly, advanced math when she was a senior. Junior was good at math, too, and Mr. Price often asked them to tutor students who were falling behind.

After math class came history. Today, things were particularly busy, with everyone using classroom resources in order to get their research papers ready for the next step—putting the information together in an organized way. Mr. Teeter had arranged for the class to meet in the library, and Crystal was soon busy at one of the eight computer terminals, reading from a tribal Web site about the Long Walk, the tribe's imprisonment at Fort Sumner, and the treaty that finally allowed the surviving Navajos to return to their homeland.

"Crystal, have you managed to find the text of the treaty signed at Fort Sumner? When was it, 1868 or 1869?"

Crystal jumped, hearing his voice directly behind her. "It was 1868, Mr. Teeter," she said. Mr.

Teeter never made much noise when he walked, but with all the computer sounds and kids whispering, he'd managed to come up right behind her this time without her ever noticing. "All I've found so far are descriptions of the agreement. The Library of Congress site was temporarily unavailable, at least that's the message I kept getting when I tried to search."

She turned her head to look at the man. The slender Anglo always dressed in a blue shirt, tan slacks, and cowboy boots. He had a narrow face, pale blue eyes, and longish hair that he combed around his ears, which made them seem to stick out even more.

"Keep looking. If you don't find an actual treaty to pick apart, pointing out the violations by both sides, your paper will lose its impact. Since it'll be difficult to change your topic now, you'd better keep at it. That paper counts for half your mark during this grading period. If you run out of time today, come by my room tomorrow morning before school and you can use the classroom computer to make another search. You don't have a computer at home, right?"

"A computer? We barely have electricity. We don't even have a phone. Don't you know that half the Navajo families around here are still living in the Stone Age?"

Crystal's mouth went dry as she suddenly realized she'd said all that out loud. The library became completely still as everyone turned to stare at her—all except Junior, who was sitting at the next table with his eyes closed, shaking his head.

Wishing that a hole would open up in the middle of the room so she could crawl into it, she sank down into her chair. One of these days she was going to learn to keep her mouth shut. Poor Junior! He was probably living the most traditional life of all the kids in their class. His mother cooked on a wood-coal stove and their home had no electricity. The only things that could have been considered modern at Junior's house were a battery-powered radio and his family's old pickup truck. She really hadn't meant to insult the lifestyle that he and his family had chosen, and that so many others here followed by necessity.

When Junior finally looked over, Crystal mouthed, *"Sorry,"* and hoped with everything in her that he'd accept her apology.

Chapter Three

WORD ABOUT what Crystal had said in the library traveled at lightning speed. By the end of third period almost everyone in school knew. Crystal could tell by the dirty looks she kept getting as she walked down the hall, even from the kids she didn't know.

The only bright spot that morning was that today the school cafeteria was serving pizza. As soon as she collected her tray, Crystal glanced around for Junior. Instead of being at their usual table in the back, he was near the exit, staring at his tray and trying his best to ignore her.

Taking a deep breath, she walked right over and stood next to him. "Is it okay if I sit here?"

"It's a free country," he growled.

"Junior, I didn't mean anything by what I said in the library. Mr. Teeter managed to get me rattled and I had an attack of stupid. That paper means a lot to my grade."

"And without good grades, you'll never get away from us Neanderthals? Navajos aren't supposed to show too much pride, but don't you think you're going a little overboard in the other direction? Running your own people down like that in front of an Anglo . . ." he said, shaking his head. "Even Teeter was embarrassed for you!"

"You don't understand," Crystal groaned.

"You've got that right." Junior finally looked up at her. "What you did—" Suddenly his gaze shifted away from her and over her shoulder to something behind her. "Don't look now, but here comes trouble—Biggins trouble."

Crystal turned around despite his warning and saw Elroy Charlie coming in their direction. Elroy's nickname was Biggins, which probably had something to do with the fact that although he was only five foot nine inches tall, he was nearly five feet wide.

"Hey, Crystal, are you sure you want to eat that Navajo pizza? It may contain dinosaur meat—maybe even Barney. I'll get rid of it for you." There were about fifty students in the cafeteria, and several laughed at his joke.

Crystal sat down quickly, thinking it would help to get the cafeteria table between her tray and the biggest football player on the team. But Biggins was quick despite his bulk. He faked a move over Crystal's left shoulder, and when she tried to push his arm away, he reached down with the other hand and snagged her slice of pizza.

"Hey, that's my lunch, Elroy." Crystal made a grab for her slice, but Biggins stepped back, and she almost fell off the bench.

Then Junior jumped to his feet, and the sound level in the cafeteria dropped sharply. Nearly all the students stopped talking and eating, and watched to see if there was going to be a fight.

"Okay, Biggins, a joke is a joke. Now how about giving her back her lunch?" Junior was nearly as tall as Elroy but weighed at least a hundred pounds less.

"And if I don't, Small-Man?" Biggins took a bite of the pizza.

"Never mind, Junior. I'll never eat pizza again," Crystal said, making a face.

"Be careful you don't choke on stolen food, Elroy Charlie," Junior whispered, deliberately using his enemy's real name. He reached into the leather medicine pouch that hung from his belt and pretended to throw something at Biggins.

Biggins flinched, then immediately started choking on the pizza. Wheezing and fighting for breath, he leaned forward and nearly vomited. At long last, he pulled the soggy mess out of his mouth.

"You want it? Take it!" he said and threw the half-chewed piece at Junior.

Junior dodged, and the thick glob plopped against a student's milk carton just as he was taking a swallow. The milk spilled down his chin and onto his shirt.

"Uh-oh," Crystal whispered, recognizing Biggin's accidental target. The student with the messy shirt was Vernon Joe, the *second* biggest kid in school. He and Biggins were the defensive tackles for the Golden Eagles.

Vernon stood, wiped the milk off his chin, then looked down at his Golden Eagles jersey. Junior eased back down onto the bench, hoping they'd forget he was even there.

Biggins and Vernon were now the only ones still standing. "You see what you did, fat boy?" Vernon headed right for Biggins.

"Drooling on your jersey again, V-J?" Biggins said, trying a joke.

Nobody laughed and Vernon kept advancing. "Hey guys, save your aggression for Kirtland Central," Crystal said, standing.

Junior tugged at Crystal's shirt sleeve. "Bad idea," he whispered urgently. "Sit down."

A second after she did, Mrs. Todacheene, the

school principal, appeared at the entrance to the cafeteria, food tray in hand. Her voice was low, cold, and deadly, and when she spoke the room temperature dropped twenty degrees. "Gentlemen, your seats or my office. Your choice."

The two football players instantly turned away from each other and went back to their seats.

Mrs. Todacheene was in her sixties and probably weighed less than ninety pounds dripping wet. Yet despite that, she was the most intimidating person Crystal had ever met. All the kids felt that way. Nobody *ever* gave her any lip, and it took great courage and a busload of stupidity even to look her in the eye.

After a few minutes, the principal turned and walked out of the cafeteria.

As soon as she'd left, Biggins walked by Junior's table on his way to the door and tried to bump him with an elbow. Junior dodged just in time.

"You won't be so lucky next time I catch you alone, Small-Man," Biggins whispered harshly.

"We'll see about that," Junior shot back. This time it was Crystal who tugged at Junior's shirt, holding him back.

"Are you crazy?" Crystal demanded as soon as Biggins left. "That big idiot can knock people down with his *thumb*. I really appreciate you sticking up for me, but his fist is as big as your head. He'll remember today and someday soon you might lose your teeth over it . . . and it'll be my fault."

"He hasn't hit me yet, so that's a win in my book. Here, have some of my pizza."

"No, don't worry about it. I still have my cottage cheese, an apple, and my milk. That's more than enough." Junior's family didn't have any more money than hers did, probably even less. Though they never would have talked about it, Crystal knew they were both in the free lunch program for low-income families. She'd noticed that, like her, he always ate everything on his tray.

"Half a pizza slice—baked by Wilma Flintstone herself. That's my final offer," Junior said.

"Well, a fourth of a slice, maybe. It wouldn't be polite to completely turn down a generous offer like that." Crystal tore his pizza into two unequal portions. Taking the smaller piece for herself, she stuck what remained into Junior's mouth. "Try not to choke like you-know-who."

"Dohn wury. Godda vig mout."

"Yes, you've got a big mouth. Me, too. But next time try to keep it closed around people who can rearrange your face, okay?"

The rest of the day wasn't so bad. After the ride home, the school bus dropped her and Junior off at the trading post.

"I've got to buy some coffee before I run home," Crystal said. "Want to come in with me?"

"Okay. I like the trading post. It always smells great in there," Junior said, following her inside. A small bell attached to the top of the door announced their presence. Mr. Albert looked up from his spot behind the counter and nodded before going back to his newspaper.

"It is kind of nice, isn't it?" Crystal commented, enjoying the scent of oiled leather from the tack and saddles, and the aroma of roasting piñon nuts coming from Mrs. Albert's old oven.

"It always feels like you've stepped into a history book," Junior said in a quiet voice. "Everything still matches my dad's stories about what things were like when he was my age—the wood-burning, potbellied stove, and that old manual cash register that rings when it opens."

"Can we pause in silence, please, for this priceless reservation moment?" Crystal announced like a preacher, then broke into a teasing grin. Her smile faded instantly when Junior didn't grin back.

Crystal nearly groaned out loud. Would she *ever* learn to keep her mouth shut? After today's slip-up, she probably shouldn't have tried to make jokes about how old-fashioned things were around here. She shrugged apologetically.

"Just get your coffee. I'll be over by the saddles. There's one I've had my eye on for months now."

As Junior moved away, Crystal went up to the trader. "I should be able to bring you my rug soon, Mr. Albert. And I want to tell you, it's turning out to be my best work ever."

"An out-of-town buyer I contacted is very interested in it. He'll be passing through Monday. If you get it to me by then I can almost guarantee you an excellent price for it. The fact that you'd dyed your own wool really sparked his interest. That makes it unique, since no two natural dyes are ever alike."

"It *is* unique—even more than you realize," she said softly. "There's no other Navajo rug like it because it has no flaw. You've heard that our people weave in a spirit line—an imperfection—as a tribute to Spider Woman, who taught the Navajos to weave?" Seeing him nod, she continued. "Mine is flawless. But please don't tell anyone around here, okay? I could get in a lot of trouble."

"Your secret will remain safe with me. And

you're right to mention it. Anything that makes your weaving one-of-a-kind allows me to ask even more money for it."

"Great!"

Crystal walked down the food aisles directly to the coffee. Although the trading post still had one of those hand grinders for the beans, it was just for show nowadays. There was an electric one for real use.

Checking the label on the brand of coffee her father preferred, she noticed the price had gone up. She couldn't afford to buy even half a pound with the money she had on her, and asking Junior for a loan was out of the question. Crystal bought a small jar of the instant instead. It was the same brand and was still selling at the old price.

Junior met her at the cash register, along with Mr. Albert, who always seemed to know where his customers were despite not having those big mirrors in the corners.

"Instant, huh?" Junior looked down at her purchase.

"Yeah. Trying to save a little time in the morning," she said, not wanting to admit she didn't have the money for the other kind.

Around here, everyone had money problems. She

remembered Lucinda telling her last week that Holly, who was on the cheerleading squad, needed a new uniform sweater. Her parents didn't have the money, and Holly was really worried that if she couldn't get the full uniform she'd have to leave the squad. Crystal counted herself lucky that she'd only needed track shoes for cross-country running, and she'd been able to find a pair the right size at a thrift shop.

"Is that all, Crystal?" Mr. Albert checked the price on the jar.

"Sure is, Mr. Albert." She smiled broadly. He grinned as he rang up the sale and took her money, showing his two gold teeth, one on each side of his upper jaw. As a kid, she'd been fascinated by the way they gleamed.

Junior nodded to Mr. Albert. "Junior," the trader acknowledged. "See you kids tomorrow."

They walked back outside, then continued together for another hundred yards or so until they reached a fork in the trail. Here, a narrow arroyo split into two smaller channels around a tall sandstone spire nearly the size of a school bus set on end. A path followed each channel, one to Junior's home, the other to hers.

Crystal stopped just before it was time for them

to go down their separate ways and grabbed Junior by the sleeve. "I just wanted to say again . . . you know . . . I'm sorry about what I said today."

He shrugged. "I know you didn't mean to hurt anyone's feelings. All your real friends know."

"So I'm forgiven?" Crystal held on to his arm longer than she ever had before.

"Uh, sure. . . . I could never stay mad at you."

Realizing how uncomfortable Junior appeared to be, she let go. The minute she did, he took a step back.

"Well, I'd better go," he said quickly. "I have homework, and I'd like to get that done before dark."

Before you have to do it by lantern or candlelight, Crystal thought with a flash of resentment. Not wanting to risk offending Junior again, all she said was, "Well, bye!"

Crystal touched her friend's hand lightly, then turned and started a slow jog down her path. After she'd gone about fifty feet, she turned her head and looked back, but Junior was gone.

Chapter Four

A HALF HOUR later Crystal was in her backyard, standing in front of her pine and cottonwood loom, which was constructed in the traditional vertical position rather than horizontally like the modern ones non-Navajos used. Her mother's voice echoed in her mind, as it always did whenever she worked on a rug. "Weaving is an extension of your inner self. Let your mind be filled with happy thoughts and show respect for your tools. Then the process will unfold with beauty and harmony."

Having begun down at the bottom of the loom, she now had to stand as she worked, since she was very close to finishing. The top of the rug represented the sky, and as the weaving took final form, she felt her spirit soar.

Crystal's fingers danced over the yarns, producing the uniform patterns of the rug. Several months ago, encouraged by how quickly he'd sold her table runners and even her small practice rugs, Mr. Albert had asked her to weave a full-size rug using a traditional design. She'd begun to work on this one right after that; when it was complete it would be four feet wide and almost six feet long.

She began to sing the weaving song her mother had taught her, to help maintain the rhythm. "In harmony and beauty, I weave," she began, her voice rich with a melody that seemed to work a magic of its own.

As she worked, Crystal thought ahead to her next step. Once she completed the rug, she'd bury it in damp sand for a few days to take out the curl. Then, after that, she'd deliver it to Mr. Albert.

As she hurried to get as much done on it as possible before sundown forced her to quit for the day, Crystal's mind filled with her vision of the perfect pattern. She'd been taught never to sketch out a design for her rugs, since that was something that had to flow from within her. Since then, she'd trained herself to see every line and every detail in her heart.

At first Crystal scarcely noticed when the air around her began to grow warm and give off a sharp odor—the kind of scent that accompanied a lightning storm. When the scent finally got her full attention, she looked around quickly, worried that she'd have to stop working soon and cover her rug.

To her surprise, the sky was cloudless and deep blue.

Then, without warning, her fingers became numb, and the strands of yarn she'd been weaving began to wobble and spin.

Crystal blinked hard, trying to get rid of the fuzzy black dot that had appeared at the center of her field of vision. But instead of disappearing, the blurred smudge seemed to grow and stand out from the fabric. Slowly, it sprouted eight long iridescent green spindly legs and an enormous human head. As the creature's gleaming eyes came into sharp focus, Crystal realized that the thing was staring right at her. Before Crystal could gather her wits, the spider spoke, its voice smooth and compelling.

"Do you know who I am?" it asked.

As she was about to answer, Crystal was startled by the loud clank of a cowbell. She looked around her and was surprised to see that she'd fallen to her knees and then, somehow, had sunk into a deep sleep.

Crystal stood and saw her father coming up the road, riding Howdie. He was following their herd of sheep and goats, which was led by an old billy goat wearing a bell around his neck.

Crystal glanced back at her loom and saw that everything looked perfectly normal now. Taking a deep, steadying breath, she tried to shake off her uneasiness. Navajo teachings warned against not leaving a spirit line, and seeing Spider Woman in her dream had unsettled her. Some of the traditionalists would have called it a warning, but she didn't believe in all that stuff. Her mother had been the tribe's best weaver, and even though she couldn't be like her mom in any other way, as a weaver Crystal knew she could measure up. Since this was her first major project, Crystal had worked hard to make it perfect—a rug worthy of all the hours her mother had spent teaching her. And the finished product would prove she could create something beautiful by being herself and making her own rules.

Crystal reached down for the canvas tarp and covered her work to protect it from the elements. Then, taking her weaving tools, she went back into the house to prepare supper.

Crystal woke up Tuesday morning in a lousy mood and wishing she could skip today altogether. Although this was her fifteenth birthday, there'd be no presents, no cake or celebration.

Louisa Manyfeathers had died on Crystal's birthday last year, and since then, she and her dad hadn't even mentioned the word *birthday*. Everything had changed after her mother's death, or had been put on hold, like her *Kinaaldá*.

When Crystal passed through the kitchen on her way outside for her run, she was surprised to see her plate was already on the table, with another plate over it to keep the food warm. Glancing out the window, she realized that her father and the animals were already gone.

Crystal picked up the note by her coffee cup and read it. Her father wanted her to know that he'd left early to go meet with Junior's dad about her *Kinaaldá*. Then, in a short P.S., he reminded her that he preferred freshly ground coffee beans to instant coffee.

Tears stinging her eyes, Crystal sat down, the note still in her hand. Her mom had been the one who'd always managed the money, and everything had been easier then. She wiped her tears away impatiently. It was precisely when dumb things like this happened that she missed her mom the most.

In a very blue mood, Crystal left for her morning run, and as she paced herself, her mind wandered back to the previous evening. She'd been taught that to fall asleep before the loom was a sign of disrespect. Her mom wouldn't have approved at all. But Crystal still had no idea how that had happened.

As she considered it, a thought occurred to her. Maybe the reason she'd had a problem was that, no matter how she tried to deny it, she still felt a little guilty for leaving out the spirit line. By falling asleep, she'd avoided finishing the rug.

That had to be it. Her dream must have been a reaction to all the pressure. There was no need to worry about it anymore.

Less than an hour later, Crystal arrived at Hudson's. Junior was in his usual place, seated at the edge of the porch, thumbing his way through his three-ringed notebook.

"Hey, Junior." She was particularly careful to avoid offending him by using his real name this morning.

"Good morning."

"I hate to bring this up, but have you decided what to do about you know who?" she asked, sitting down beside him. After the incident with Biggins, she'd really hoped Junior would be absent today. But she couldn't remember the last time he'd missed school—for any reason.

"Biggins? Well, you know how a lot of Navajos believe there's power in a name, and if you use it too much, you weaken that person?" Junior asked.

"Yeah, so?" Crystal put her book bag down, then

sat beside him, their legs almost touching.

Junior squirmed just a little but didn't move his leg. "I must have said 'Elroy Charlie' a thousand times on the way here this morning. Hope it works."

"And if it doesn't?"

"To quote Muhammad Ali, 'I'm going to float like a butterfly and sting like a bee.'"

"Please, no poetry this early in the morning." Crystal rolled her eyes.

"Shorty said he'd back me up," Junior added, ignoring her.

"Scrape you up is more like it," she mumbled. "Why don't you just stay out of the cafeteria?"

"Because I like to eat. And besides, I'm not about to let anyone bully me."

"Then break some school rule third period so you'll be sent to the office. They still have to bring you a tray and allow you to eat, but you can avoid a fight."

"Aw, come on. Neither of us has ever been sent to the office. We don't have a clue what happens during lunch in there."

"What is it with boys and all that manly warrior posturing?" Crystal grabbed his arm and held on tightly. "You could get seriously hurt. Find a way to avoid a fight, at least for today. By tomorrow he'll have forgotten all about you. The pea brain inside that di—I mean moose—is incapable of storing information for very long."

"Ha! You were going to say dinosaur, weren't you? Got the Stone Age on your mind again?" Junior teased.

"Don't remind me, and quit changing the subject."

"Too late, here comes the bus."

"Where? I don't hear anything." Crystal looked down the road. It was empty.

"Wait for it . . . there."

Sure enough, the bus came up out of a low spot in the road just then. Crystal looked curiously at Junior, but he just smiled.

Crystal hurried into math, her first-period class. She'd been able to do a little research at Mr. Teeter's computer before the bell, but the printer had been slow, and she'd barely made it here in time.

Crystal reached into her backpack and brought out her notebook. A small piece of paper folded in half fell out of it.

She opened it quickly.

Happy Birthday, Daughter.

The three words made her stomach feel hollow, and guilt settled over her like a heavy weight.

Things were just as difficult for her father today as they were for her. Yet he'd still taken the time to do something nice for her. Tears welling up in her eyes, she reached for a tissue from her purse and looked around to see if anyone had noticed her crying. That's when she saw Junior watching her.

Grumbling about allergies loud enough for even Mr. Price to hear, she sat up straight and slipped the note into her purse. The rest of math class was pleasant, almost cheerful.

A little over an hour later, Crystal stood beside Mr. Teeter's desk as he thumbed through the rough draft of her report on treaties.

"Your work, as usual, is excellent, and you've recorded the history of these documents and their content clearly and concisely. But the human element is missing—not only the reactions of the individuals involved and the tribes, but your own analysis and evaluation as well."

"You mean what the tribes thought of the treaties, and how they reacted when the terms weren't honored? That's the analysis part, right?" Crystal said.

"Yes. In addition to the traditional, academic research you've done, I want you to take it a step further. I'd like to see your personal evaluation included in this. I don't just want to know what the people involved back then thought. For instance, tell me what you think should have been included or left out of the treaties and why," Mr. Teeter said, looking at her. "That shouldn't be too tough for you. You've never held back your opinion before, have you?" he added with a teasing smile.

"What could I possibly say that would make any difference? This is history. It's already happened and there's nothing we can do about it—not without a time machine, anyway."

"Why do you think we study history? It's not just to give old folks a reason for writing their memoirs. If we learn from the past, we can hopefully keep from making the same mistakes in the future. Getting back to your project, do you understand what I'd like you to add to make it more meaningful to you?"

She nodded, then returned to her desk.

For the rest of the morning, Crystal had little to say to anyone, applying herself to her work and going from one class to the next in a moody daze.

It wasn't until she was going through the lunch line that she remembered Junior's impending doom. Recalling that she'd seen him somewhere ahead of her in line, she rushed to find him the minute she got her tray, hoping he was in his regular spot.

"Junior!" she yelled as soon as she saw him, and several people looked up.

"Bad idea," she mumbled, realizing that she'd just drawn attention to him. As she hurried over to join him, her canned peaches sloshed over the side of the tray, and she spilled some of the syrup onto the cafeteria floor. "Rats!"

"Hi, Birdie. I saved you a place," Junior said. "You spilled stuff on the floor. Did you know that?"

"Yeah, I'd better go back and clean it up." She put down her tray and looked over toward the opening where they turned in their trays. As usual, a mop and bucket were there ready for use.

Before she could go get the mop, a loud voice broke through the low murmur of conversations.

"Small-Man!" Biggins turned and handed his plastic tray heaped with food to the student behind him, who happened to be Shorty. "Hold this, kid. I won't take long," he said.

Biggins walked straight toward them, a scowl on his face and his fists doubled up.

"Wait," Crystal said, trying to warn him about the wet spot on the floor—but it was too late.

Biggins's shoe came down onto the puddle of peach syrup, and an instant later, his leg flew up into the air. The heavy football player seemed to hover endlessly; then, as gravity took control, he crashed to the floor with a mighty thud.

Crystal started to smile at the thought of the big bully getting what he deserved, but Junior glanced at her and shook his head. "Don't do it. Do you want to die?" he whispered.

Biggins began to groan, and a half dozen boys rushed to help him up.

"Back off!" Biggins yelled, grimacing in pain as he held his arm at an unnatural angle.

Feeling guilty that he was really hurt and it was partially her fault that he'd fallen, Crystal ignored his anger and went to offer him a hand up. "Here, let me help," she said with a tentative smile.

He accepted her gesture with his uninjured hand, then almost pulled her down with him because of the difference in their weights. Junior and Shorty ran up and anchored her in place long enough for Biggins to stand upright.

Just then Mrs. Todacheene came into the cafeteria. "What's going on here?" she demanded, looking around. Noticing the strange color on Biggins's face and the awkward way he was holding his injured arm, she added, "What happened to you?"

"He slipped and fell," Crystal volunteered.

Biggins nodded.

"Let's have the nurse take a look at your arm,

Mr. Charlie," Mrs. Todacheene said, motioning with her head for him to follow her.

As soon as Biggins was out of the cafeteria, people began to talk again, but in low whispers in case Biggins could somehow still hear them.

Shorty set both his and Biggins's tray down. "Anyone for seconds?"

"I'm not going to eat his food, and I don't think you should either," Crystal said. "What if he sends someone back for it?"

"At least Junior's safe for now," Holly said. "That is, unless Elroy can beat him up with just one hand."

Crystal looked at Shorty and then they both turned to Junior, who'd remained silent.

"I'd better start praying that they serve peaches every day this year, or I'm a dead man," Junior said at last.

Chapter Five

THAT AFTERNOON Crystal arrived home early, having run almost all the way from Hudson's. The clean, fresh air and the familiar scent of sagebrush and pine, so much stronger here than around the school, had revitalized her. It occurred to her that she'd really miss those two things when she finally moved away.

Sobered by the thought, she left her school bag on the couch, went outside, then uncovered the loom and began weaving again. Yesterday's unscheduled nap had interrupted her work, and she was anxious to complete the rug today before her father got home.

Crystal concentrated on her work, wanting to make sure that the finished end of the rug was as thick as the beginning, a sign of quality. She'd been working for about two hours and had nearly finished the rug, when she suddenly felt light-headed. Then, right before her eyes, the colored yarns began to vibrate and swirl, weaving impossible patterns in the air. In the center of it all was the same dark spot she'd seen the day before. It spiraled slowly, then faster, until it was just a black blur.

This time no giant spider became visible, but the same smooth, compelling voice she'd heard before began speaking to her.

"You know what I want. Is it so hard for you to show respect?" the feminine voice asked.

"Hey, Earth calling Birdie! Come in, Birdie!" another more familiar voice piped in.

Feeling someone shaking her shoulders, Crystal came fully awake. "Junior? What . . . Aw, rats. It happened again," she muttered, standing up. "I have no idea why I keep falling asleep every time I weave." She brushed the hair out of her eyes, looked back at the rug, and told him about her strange dreams.

"Are you feeling okay right now?" Junior asked.

"I'm fine."

"Good, 'cause I've got a surprise for you." With a tentative smile, Junior reached into his pocket and brought out a small leather pouch with a drawstring closure on the top. "It's a gift—something I wanted you to have today," he said, avoiding the word *birthday* altogether. "I know you didn't want to celebrate, but I thought this might be okay with you."

She took the pouch and saw that it had been hand beaded in the pattern of a running antelope. The leather was as soft as velvet. "It's a beautiful medicine pouch! Thank you so much!"

"You can use it for carrying sacred items, like turquoise, flint, white shell, and special tokens. Or you can just stick spare change in it—whatever you want. I'm not trying to push the Navajo Way on you. Really. I just wanted to make you something that was special. . . ." Junior looked down at his shoes.

"It's a wonderful gift and I love it." Crystal gave him a quick hug, then stepped back as he looked up in surprise.

"I've always thought of you . . . ever since we were kids . . . you know . . . as special. . . ." Junior was having trouble speaking all of a sudden.

"I'll keep this forever," Crystal said.

For several moments an awkward silence stretched out between them. "Hey, why don't you take a picture of me with my new medicine pouch?" Crystal said, anxious to change the subject. "I think there's still some film in my camera." She ran toward the house before he could answer.

A few minutes later Junior was looking through the viewfinder of the camera, trying to decide on where to pose Crystal. Finally he decided. "Stand in front of your rug. It's beautiful, and it says something about you and what you are."

"Yeah. Something you made, something I made. Good idea," Crystal said. "Okay, how's this?" She stood in front of the loom, held up the medicine pouch, then smiled. He snapped the shutter.

"Take another. That one will be for you."

Junior did, then handed her the camera. "So tell me, what are you going to do about those dreams? You can't just ignore stuff like that, Birdie."

She exhaled softly, suddenly regretting having told him. "They're just nightmares, nothing to worry about."

"In the Anglo world that may be true, but we're Navajo." Junior sat down on the ground beside the loom. "You should sprinkle your house and yourself with corn pollen. Then sing some Good Luck Songs to drive those dark dreams away."

He paused for several moments, but she fiddled with the camera, not saying a word. "Birdie, I don't want you to think I'm trying to tell you what to do, or passing judgment. You have to follow your own path, even if it leads away from here for a while. But this new problem could really get in the way of your future. I hope you're not planning to just ignore this."

She shrugged. “What can be done?”

“There are some options you can consider. I think you’ve been seeing Spider Woman, and she’s a serious power. Even though you’re determined to adopt the Anglo ways, you’re still Navajo and that means you have to follow the rules laid down for our people.” He stared at her rug, lost in thought. “You *did* put in a spirit line, didn’t you?” Junior stepped closer to the rug, checking the pattern.

“You might as well stop looking,” she said, shaking her head.

Junior groaned. “I’m *sure* you were warned about Blanket Sickness and Spider Woman when you first learned to weave. If you omit the tribute due her, Spider Woman will weave cobwebs in your mind and trap your thoughts inside the pattern of your rug. Why would you ignore that—particularly after Spider Woman herself came to warn you?”

“This is my first big project and the best work I’ve ever done! I carded the wool, spun it, and even dyed it myself. This is *my* creation. I won’t do something to purposely make it less than perfect—and I shouldn’t have to.” She paused, then in a soft voice added, “What’s really crazy is that even though I don’t think I’ve done anything really wrong, I still feel a little guilty because I didn’t do things the way my mom would have done them.”

"The fact that you do feel guilty should tell you something. Now your mind and body aren't in harmony, and that's what leads to sickness. You should have a Sing done right away. By fighting our ways, you're fighting yourself. You have to restore your *hozho*—your harmony."

"I'll talk to my father about it." Crystal looked at her watch. It had stopped, and from what she could see, this had happened right about the time she'd finished weaving. "This is strange," she said, and showed him the watch.

"Spider Woman is still trying to get your attention. She's giving you a chance to make things right before you take the rug off the loom. Unless you pay attention to her now, Birdie, you may lose your ability to weave forever."

Maybe Junior had a point. If she fell asleep every single time she tried to weave, it would be nothing short of a disaster. But she still had her doubts. "I don't know about this. . . ."

"Then let's go see my dad. You can listen to what he has to say, then make up your own mind."

"Okay." Maybe this would help her stop feeling guilty, and then things would return to normal. "But I want you to know that I'm only doing this because I want to be able to weave without having all these crazy dreams."

Twenty minutes later they arrived at Junior's home, a small wood-framed building with a pitched roof and a pale blue stucco exterior. On the west side of the house was a shed for the chickens and ducks, a corral with three covered stalls for the horses, and a larger arena where other livestock could be contained at night and during bad weather.

Fifty yards to the east of the house was the medicine hogan where Junior's father worked. It was a six-sided structure built of big pine logs with a rounded roof with a smoke hole in the center. The entrance was covered by a heavy wool blanket that served as the door.

"We'll wait here until my dad comes out and invites us to approach," Junior said.

She knew that it was just polite to wait for an invitation, but now that she was here, she wanted to get on with it. "Maybe we can make some noise just to let him know we're here, you know?"

"He knows. Be patient."

"How do you know he knows?"

A heartbeat later, Henry Tallman, Senior, came to the entrance and waved at them.

"Someday, Junior, you're going to have to tell me how you do that," she muttered.

Henry Senior was in his forties and had an

imposing appearance. His black hair was tinged with gray at the temples and touched his shoulders. He wore a white headband—the trademark of a *hataalii*—and a flannel shirt and jeans. Attached to his leather belt was a worn medicine pouch that looked a bit like the one Junior had given to Crystal.

"Sit down," he said as they entered, motioning them to sheepskins placed on the hard-packed dirt floor.

For a moment Crystal panicked. She knew that women were supposed to sit in a certain location and men in another. A third spot was reserved for the medicine man. But at that precise moment she didn't have a clue as to which was which.

Junior, sensing her panic, pointed her to the north side of the small fire burning in the pit at the center of the hogan.

The *hataalii* sat in the place of honor—on the west and opposite the entrance. After his father was seated, Junior lowered himself onto the sheepskin on the south side of the hogan.

"Now tell me what has brought you here today," the *hataalii* asked.

Junior looked at Crystal and, seeing her nod, explained to his father what had happened.

"You don't follow many of the traditional ways,"

the *hataalii* said to Crystal, "but you *are Dineh*—Navajo—and you now have a problem that needs to be fixed. Harmony has to be restored."

Crystal nodded, afraid to say anything. The last thing she needed was to irritate the medicine man.

When she didn't speak, the *hataalii* smiled. "You're afraid of saying the wrong thing and making me angry, but that's the least of your problems right now."

Crystal sighed. Now she knew where Junior got his abilities. They both did more than talk—they observed and saw things that ordinary people missed. "I feel guilty for going against my mother's teaching. Now I'm having crazy dreams, and I don't like any of this," she said.

"You're not walking in beauty. Do you know what that means?"

She nodded. "I'm not living in harmony with all the things that make up my life."

"And in your case it's not just disharmony—you're at war," he added with a little smile.

"I know what I want and what it'll take to get me there," she said. "That doesn't exactly put me at war. I'd say it makes me stubborn and determined."

The words came out of her mouth before she'd had time to think, and now she was afraid even to look in the direction of the medicine man. She'd probably blown sky-high her chances of getting any help. Junior would never speak to her again.

When she heard Mr. Tallman chuckle, she breathed a silent sigh of relief. "I'm sorry. Sometimes things don't come out quite the way I mean them," she said softly.

"I appreciate your honesty—but you could try to be more diplomatic," he added.

Not hearing any trace of anger in his voice gave her courage. "Can you fix things for me so I can weave in peace?"

"Fix? I can sing a Blessing Song for you, but *you* must take responsibility for fixing the problem."

Crystal exhaled softly. "Put in a spirit line, right?"

"Yes, that too. But even before that, you must show Spider Woman the proper respect, and you also need to honor Beautiful Flowers. She's the Chief of all Medicines."

"How do I do that?" Crystal asked immediately, then realized that she'd interrupted Mr. Tallman. Frustrated, she stared at her hands and hoped he wasn't angry. "I'm going to be quiet now. If you want me to say anything, just let me know, okay?" She glanced up at him and smiled weakly.

His eyes were laughing despite his otherwise serious expression, and it was a moment before he finally spoke. "Find one chip of turquoise and one of white shell, then take them to your family's shrine. Give the turquoise to Spider Woman as an offering. Then leave the white shell offering inside the petals of the loveliest flower you can find for Beautiful Flowers." He looked at his son. "Sing a Good Medicine Song for her after the offering is made," he said, then looked back at Crystal. "Do you understand what needs to be done?"

She nodded but, remembering her promise, said nothing.

"The offering will be the easy part for you, I have a feeling," the *hataalii* said. "When you return home—before you take the rug off the loom—you must put in a spirit line."

Crystal nodded and remained quiet, thinking. She'd do the offering for sure and, with luck, that would be enough.

"A lot of cultures pay tribute to their gods this way," he explained. "In Kashmir, almost an entire world away, weavers always work a flaw into their work. It's their way of honoring their belief that only Allah is perfect. Other Indian tribes in our country follow similar practices. But it all comes down to one thing—respect."

Crystal nodded thoughtfully, considering what he'd said.

"Now I'm going to do a pollen blessing over you."

The *hataalii* lifted his voice in song, praising the four sacred mountains. The vibrant chant seemed to charge the air around them with power, and she was surprised when her heart began to drum with excitement. The *hataalii*'s voice grew strong and she was spellbound, captured by each syllable. When the song grew softer, she found herself mesmerized by each note and uplifted by the sound itself.

At the close of the song, the *hataalii* opened his medicine bag, touched the corn pollen to the tip of his tongue and to the top of his head, then threw the rest into the air above him. As pollen rained gently down on them, Crystal knew that something wonderful had just happened. She couldn't explain it, and she certainly hadn't suddenly become a believer in Navajo ways, but the good feeling persisted.

"Now you have questions," Mr. Tallman said at the end, and nodded to her.

Crystal swallowed to relieve the dryness in her throat, but it didn't help. "What just happened? You didn't give me any medicine or anything, yet I feel . . . good."

"Navajo healers believe that all things are interconnected. In order to heal the body we believe it's necessary to heal the spirit first."

"Psychology, you mean?" Crystal asked.

"It's much more than that. The Navajo Way—the path of the traditionalists—also relies on our connection to the Holy People and what they taught us," the *hataalii* said.

He looked at her for several moments. "But I can see that's raised another question—a troubling one. Go ahead, ask."

"If that spiritual connection is there and the Navajo gods are so all-powerful, then why is it that the *Dineh* still have awful things like poverty, and death?" she blurted, then cringed. "I should have stayed quiet, huh?"

The healer smiled. "Your question is perfectly reasonable, and you deserve an answer." Mr. Tallman took a long, deep breath, then began. "At the time of the beginning, Sun married Turquoise Woman and they had two sons—Slayer and his twin brother, Child-of-the-Water." His voice deepened and grew strong, compelling her to listen. "It was a time of great danger, when monsters preyed upon the earth, and the two boys grew up knowing hard times. But their experiences toughened them physically and mentally. Eventually they became fierce warriors. One day they set out together to rid the land of evil."

The *hataalii*'s voice filled the hogan, and as he told his story, the words came alive in Crystal's mind, creating images much more vivid than those on any movie screen.

"Then, just when the Hero Twins thought that their job was finished, and that the earth was finally safe, they came across four pitiful-looking strangers—Cold, Hunger, Poverty, and Death," he said. "The warriors, anxious to finish their quest, set out to destroy them, but before they could, each asked to be heard and allowed to state their case for being spared. The Twins consented."

"They should have just killed them," Crystal muttered.

The *hataalii* smiled, then continued. "Cold was the first to speak. She was a thin woman in a threadbare dress with only rags to cover her feet. She warned that if she died, it would be hot all year round. There would be no snow, and without it the lakes and rivers would dry up. So the Hero Twins allowed her to live.

"Then Hunger, a skeletal man, spoke and explained that with his death, the people would lose their appetites. Without him, no one would ever experience the pleasure of roast lamb, warm corn bread, or even a slice of juicy melon. The people would grow lazy because they wouldn't need to grow their food or care for livestock." He paused and looked at her. "And that's why Hunger was allowed to exist."

"But what about the other two? Poverty and Death? Surely neither of those had anything good to offer," Crystal said.

"When the Hero Twins turned to Poverty, an old woman dressed in rags, she explained that without her, no one would ever have a reason or the energy to better themselves, and eventually, the people would die in spirit. And that's why she was allowed to live."

Positive that no logic would excuse death—at least as far as she was concerned—Crystal waited for his last explanation.

"Finally, they faced Death. Without her, the skeletal figure explained, the old people wouldn't give up their places to the young. The cycle of life would stop, and pretty soon there wouldn't be enough room for everyone. The land would be barren and crowded. She explained that she was their friend, though they didn't realize it."

"Death took away my mother and has almost destroyed my family," Crystal said. "They should have killed her."

"The loss of your mother could have brought you and your father closer together, but you've refused to allow that to happen. Death isn't completely responsible for your unhappiness now," he said gently. "Your anger is what keeps you alone—what makes you hate being Navajo."

"My mother should have been in a hospital!" Crystal said, tears stinging her eyes.

"Her illness came on suddenly," the *hataalii* explained patiently. "I saw your mother that day. She'd come to me for a blessing because she *was* getting ready to go to the public health hospital. She'd had a headache for days. I was worried about her too, so while your father drove us all to the hospital I did the blessing on the way. You were out running cross-country that morning, remember? That's why you weren't there to go with us."

Crystal began to tremble as the memories rushed back. She'd known her mom hadn't been feeling well. She should have stayed at home and maybe even forced her to go to the hospital sooner.

"The doctors said she'd had an aneurism—a blood vessel had swollen up and burst in her brain. No one could have predicted that," the *hataalii* added, as if he'd read her mind.

"One of the Twins should have killed Death," Crystal whispered.

"Your mother's memory lives on through the knowledge and skill she passed on to you. That's a very rich legacy."

Crystal saw him exchange a quick look with Junior. Once again she got the strange feeling that those closest to her shared a secret they were keeping from her. Before she could say anything, he continued.

"Actions always have consequences. By not making the spirit line that honored Spider Woman and your own heritage, you've started a chain of events. Now it's up to you to make things right."

Junior's father stood up, signaling that it was time for them to go. "Thank you, uncle," Crystal said, using the term out of respect, not kinship.

As they walked out of the hogan, Crystal felt more confident than she had before. With a plan in mind, things never seemed quite as hopeless.

The sun had already set by the time they headed back to Crystal's home, both of them on Junior's horse. Anxious to get home before dark, they'd taken a shortcut that led them across a wide, flat meadow punctuated by tufts of straw-colored grass and low, gray-green rabbitbrush.

"What do you think of my father's advice,

Birdie?" Junior kept his gaze forward, guiding the long-maned quarter horse with a light touch on the reins. Arrow was a five-year-old gelding who wouldn't spook at anything less than a bear in the trail.

"He's a smart man. He knows a lot about a whole bunch of things. He should have gone to college—no offense about what he's doing now, okay?"

"None taken, I know what you mean. My father is always surprising me by talking about things I've never even heard about," Junior said. "And, by the way, he did go to college. He got a bachelor's degree at Stanford, and lived in California for a few years afterward. Then he decided to come home."

"Why? He could have been anything he wanted to be."

Junior smiled.

"You know what I mean."

"Yeah, I do. Dad says that he returned because it was what was best for him and for the *Dineh*. As a *hataalii* he could practice healing ways that the white world is only just beginning to discover. Until recently, Anglo doctors didn't understand that *both* the body and mind needed to be healed." Junior paused then added, "Dad says that our country assimilates cultures—brings them together as one—

and that's not bad. But it's our Navajo beliefs that make us who we are, and it's through them that our tribe remains strong."

"I'm not really sure I agree with all that, but I'm going to follow his advice. If I can get rid of my nightmares by leaving offerings for Spider Woman and Beautiful Flowers, I'm all for it." She kept both her arms wrapped around Junior as they rode. She'd always loved riding double with him.

"You'll also have to rework the rug and put in a spirit line," he reminded her.

"One step at a time," she said. "Maybe the offerings will be enough."

He turned his head and glared at her. "I can't believe you just said that. If you want to get out of this mess, Birdie, you're going to have to do both—and fast."

"Let's see what happens after I make the offerings. The place your father told us to visit is one that always brings good luck to my family."

Crystal had heard the family story many times. One of her ancestors had been sheltered from freezing weather there and had survived subzero conditions. After that he'd built a four-foot-high cairn of rocks, twigs, and bits of turquoise and had sung a Good Luck Song that had become her family's special prayer.

When silence stretched out between them, Crystal realized that Junior was still angry with her. Trying to distract him, she said, “I’ve been meaning to ask you something, Junior. How did you manage to make Biggins choke on the pizza, or step right into the peach syrup? How do you know the bus is coming before either of us hears or sees it? Are you some kind of magician?”

“Magician? No. But I am learning a few things from my father. Being a *hataalii* requires special knowledge.”

“That still doesn’t answer my question.” She waited, but Junior remained quiet. “You’re not going to tell me, are you?”

“How about that? You can read *my* mind. Now hang on. We have a little ditch to jump.”

Chapter Six

AS THEY approached Crystal's home, deep shadows filled the canyons and draped the steep slopes of the mesas. Although traditional Navajos said that this was a dangerous time—that the darkness often hid evil—this was the time of day she loved the best. The workday was finished, and peaceful quiet settled over everything. Only the low murmur of the night insects accented the stillness around them.

Junior pulled back lightly on the reins and Arrow stopped near the peeled cottonwood branch corral, which was half filled with sheep. Crystal slid down the animal's left side onto the soft ground, then Junior dismounted.

"Will you put in the spirit line now?" Junior pressed.

"First I'm going to find the turquoise and white shell I need and make the offering. After that's done, I'll deal with the rug. Right now I'm just going to cover the loom with the tarp. I should have done that before I left, but I didn't think we'd be gone this long."

Before he had the chance to argue with her, Crystal ran around the side of the house. Suddenly her heart froze and her breath caught in her throat. Unable to utter a word, she pointed at the loom.

"Where's your rug?" Junior asked, coming around the corner.

"It's gone!" she managed at last. As she stepped up to the loom, she saw that the dowels that held the rug had been cut away from the top and bottom beams. "It's been taken—and not carefully either," she said, her voice trembling. "There are tufts of yarn on the ground. If you tell me Spider Woman did this, I'll scream!"

"No, this was the work of a human, that's for sure," he answered calmly.

Crystal couldn't stop shaking. "Who would do this to me?"

"Maybe your father—"

Not giving him a chance to finish, Crystal raced into the house. Only silence greeted her.

"The pickup is gone, didn't you notice?" Junior came into the kitchen.

Spotting a note on the table, she read it quickly. "He's making last-minute arrangements for the

Kinaaldá. Dad must have come home, put the animals away, then left again. But he wouldn't have taken my rug and not said anything," she said, turning the note over but finding no other message.

Panic gripped her. She'd used all her skill and experience weaving that rug and had spent months and months working on it. Now it was possible that the thief had damaged it—or worse, that she might never see it again.

Crystal burst into tears of frustration. "This is crazy! No one could possibly hate me *that* much."

"You'll need to think clearly now, so try to relax."

"Relax? Are you nuts? Someone took my rug!"

"If you want your rug back, you'd better get yourself together," he snapped.

Something in Junior's tone broke through her fear and captured her attention. Though her hands were still shaking, Crystal forced herself to take a deep breath and struggled to calm down.

Finally she looked up. "Okay," she said, forcing herself to look composed, though that wasn't even close to the way she really felt. "First, we have to figure out who took it. Then, we'll go get it back." The words made her start shaking all over again, this time from anger. "Do you think all this could just be a prank? Maybe someone took the rug from the loom and left it someplace else for me to find."

Lighting two big kerosene lanterns, they searched everywhere, including the sheep pen, but weren't able to find the rug anywhere.

"This is starting to look really bad, Birdie. I don't think this was a prank," he said.

Crystal bit back her tears, determined to come up with a plan. "We *have* to find it. But I don't even know where to start looking!"

"There are a lot of potential suspects," he said. "You've ticked off a lot of people recently."

"I know, I know. But if it's one of the kids at school, they'll eventually say or do something to give themselves away. I'm sure of it."

As they walked around the corral, the bright circles of light from their lanterns chased the dark shadows away, giving them a clear look at the ground. "Look at those tracks," she said, pointing just ahead to a spot in front of the house.

"A truck pulling a horse trailer was parked there," he said, studying the marks closely. "They circled completely around the house to turn around. See the second set of tire tracks separated from the first set? That's where the hitch would be." Junior glanced around quickly. "All the animals are here, right?"

"I didn't count the sheep, but none of them appear to be missing, and the other animals, saddles, and tack are here. The house is just as I left it, too."

While she took a closer look at the tracks, Junior walked across the yard to where the loom was set up. As he lowered the lantern, the area was bathed in a soft bright light.

"I hadn't checked before, but there are footprints here that aren't yours or mine," he called out to her. "Also the person who was near this loom wore boots with pointed toes."

Crystal rushed up, adding the light from her lantern as well. "Then they definitely don't belong to my dad. He's got an old pair of boots, but they have a squared-off toe." She paused, fighting the frustration that bit at her. "But I have no idea what good those footprints are going to do us, or the truck and trailer tracks. The trail stops at the road, and since that's hard ground, it's impossible to say where the person went."

"If we can narrow down the list of people who might have taken the rug, we may be able to use this information to identify the guilty person. But we need to preserve these tracks."

"How?"

"My dad has been teaching me how to create sandpaintings—just simple designs so I can develop my skill, not real ones. But sometimes the wind destroyed my work before Dad could take a look. We came up with a way to preserve them, using a mixture of starch and water, or sugar and water if it's winter and there's no chance that bugs will get on it. Both ways moisten the soil, then dry, holding everything in place."

A short time later, after raiding the kitchen, they returned with a spray bottle containing the starch and water mixture, and a large piece of cardboard. Working carefully, they saturated the impressions with the spray, then waited until the ground was stiff enough to allow them to slide the sections of tracks onto the cardboard sheet without crumbling.

"Keep this someplace safe," Junior said, handing it over to her.

"I know just the place." Crystal carried it into the house while Junior opened the doors ahead of her. Finally she slid it beneath her bed. "It'll be fine there."

As they walked back outside, Crystal glanced at Junior. "I was thinking about who might have done this and one name suddenly popped into my head—Biggins."

"I was just thinking the same thing," Junior admitted. "He's mean enough, but I don't know if he wears pointed boots, or how big they are. Also, with his injured arm, I'm not sure if he's capable of driving, let alone taking the rug off the loom with just one hand."

"Good point," she said, considering the matter.

"Maybe a neighbor who'd seen you working on the rug decided to take it. Or you could have had a regular, everyday, run-of-the-mill thief. He didn't see anything he wanted in the house, but taking the rug more than made up for his time."

Hating the new thought that formed in her mind, Crystal added, "Mr. Albert has been very eager to get this rug so he can sell it. But he wouldn't . . . would he?"

"I don't think so, but we should look into that possibility anyway," Junior said.

"He was really excited when I told him that it was unique because—" She stopped, realizing what Junior's reaction would be.

Junior's dark eyes bored into her. "You didn't tell *him* that you hadn't put in a spirit line, did you?"

"Yeah, I did," she replied, then sighed. "I just wanted him to know how different it was from anyone else's work."

"That was the worst idea you've ever had—and, Birdie, that's saying a lot!"

"Does that mean you think he might have stolen it?"

"All I know is that we need to check it out."

"I've got to get it back before this weekend, Junior. I don't have a rug dress to wear for the ceremony. Those are really expensive and we can't afford it. It takes special skills to weave the pieces and fashion them into a garment. So I was planning to use my rug as a shawl."

"Without a spirit line?"

"I'm going through the *Kinaaldá* for my dad, but using that rug during the ceremony—well, that was for me. It was my declaration of independence. I may be part of the tribe, but I'm an individual, too." She paused, then added, "And just so you know, I did ask Mr. Albert not to tell anyone around here that my rug didn't have a spirit line. I warned him that it would create lots of problems."

"Birdie, every time I think I might be close to understanding you . . ." he said, shaking his head.

"You don't need to understand me. Just keep being my friend and help me get my rug back."

"I'm already doing that. But what about telling your dad? Maybe he can help."

"No," she said firmly. "He has more than enough to do getting things ready for the ceremony. He's been working awfully long hours just to iron out all the details, and I don't want to give him something else to worry about now. I won't lie to him, but I'll let him believe that I buried the rug in the sand to take out the curl. If we haven't found the rug by Friday, then I'll tell him the truth."

"Have you thought about the possibility that maybe somebody in the trading post overheard Mr. Albert telling a potential buyer what made your rug so unique? If that happened then the thief could be someone out to punish you for not following traditional ways."

"That could be it," Crystal said. She mulled things over for several moments, then continued. "The first thing we should do is decide where to start our search, and I have an idea. I don't think Mr. Albert has a horse trailer—at least I've never seen one parked where he leaves his truck and he doesn't have any horses. So let's get up extra early tomorrow and go by Biggins's house before the school bus arrives. Biggins has a pickup, and if we see him driving despite his injury, then it's possible he may have been the one who took the rug. We could also check to see if his family has a horse trailer."

"Okay, you're on." Junior looked back at Arrow. "I'd better be getting back or Mom will start to worry."

"Okay, but Junior, we can't tell *anyone* that my rug was stolen. If everyone starts looking for it—

particularly the police—whoever has it will get rid of it permanently so they won't get caught and I'll never see it again."

"But the thief is sure to know that you'll be looking for it," he answered.

"Yes, and with luck, he'll wonder what's going on and why I haven't told anyone. That'll distract him and he might slip up. Or maybe he'll think that I'm afraid to tell anyone because I hadn't added a spirit line. In either case, it's going to keep him guessing."

"You'd better hope the thief lives around here and your rug is still in the area."

"Yeah, I know," she said somberly.

"Let's meet tomorrow at the crossroads."

"How about at daybreak?"

He nodded. "After prayers to the dawn, yes."

"I will never understand you, either, Junior," she muttered.

He mounted the horse effortlessly, then looked back down at her. "The Navajo Way is *real*, Birdie. It can support you when things go wrong and make you stronger than you ever thought you could be. But it takes effort to learn our ways, and confidence to start relying on them."

"I'm doing my best to learn what I need to so I

can make it through the *Kinaaldá*. I'm supposed to bake a cake in the ground and lay the batter over a sheet of corn husks I've sewn together. But I'm not really good at sewing, and I'm afraid everything will just leak through and I'll have a giant mess instead of a cake. And the stirring sticks—the *ádístsiin*—are impossible to work with. They're greasewood sticks tied together, for pete's sake. Why not just use a spoon? And I have to sing the prayers, which go on and on. I do know most of those already, but I'm afraid I'll totally blank out when it's time."

"Are you prepared for *anything*?"

She smiled and nodded. "Well, I can run. Racing for half a mile is nothing."

"What will you do about the rest? Saturday is only a couple of days away."

"One way or another I'll learn what I need to by then. I want my dad to remember my *Kinaaldá* with pride, even long after I'm gone."

"You're looking at your ceremony all wrong," he said patiently.

"It is what it is, and I am what I am," she answered.

Junior started to argue, then stopped. "Find what you need to make the offering to Spider Woman and Beautiful Flowers like my dad told you. Then, as soon as you're ready, we'll go to your family's shrine." He looked up at the darkening skies. "I'd better get going," he said and loped off.

As she watched Junior ride away, Crystal thought about the offering. She had a chip of turquoise and one of white shell in her dresser. Although she didn't really want to part with them, she would. One way or another, she had to stop falling asleep in front of the loom. And if the person who'd stolen her rug had done so to punish her for her nontraditional ways, maybe word would reach him that she'd seen a *hataalii* and was following his orders. If she got lucky, maybe that would persuade him to return her rug.

As she went back inside the empty house, sadness enveloped her. Home had been so different when her mom had been alive. Even though she and her mother had often disagreed on things, they'd always been friends.

Her mom, like her dad, had been a traditionalist. Weaving had only been one part of the lifestyle and beliefs her mother had wanted her to accept. That was why, along with the craft, Crystal had been taught all the weaving songs and the stories about Spider Woman.

Somehow, when her mother had been alive, everything had been easier to believe and accept. She'd done as her mother had asked back then, but she was no longer a child. Her *Kinaaldá* was only three days away. She had a right to do things her own way.

Crystal went to the kitchen and turned on the light. It was past time to prepare supper, but it really didn't matter tonight because her father was going to be late. The mutton stew she'd fixed yesterday would make great leftovers. She'd just finished warming up the big pot when her father finally drove up in the pickup.

When he joined her at the table, Crystal noticed that he seemed more tired than usual. They didn't speak at all until after he'd finished his meal.

"How's the rug coming?" he asked, leaning back in his chair.

Crystal's throat tightened. Of all the times for him to ask! "I hope I'll be able to show it to you on Saturday," she said carefully, then stood and began to gather up the dirty dishes. Ten minutes later she slipped into her bedroom—a question-free zone.

Crystal sat on the bed, fiddling with *ádístsiin*, the mush sticks for stirring. Knowing she'd need to get a feel for how they worked prior to the ceremony, Crystal's Aunt Atlnaba had loaned these to her. The special favor hadn't been lost on Crystal. She knew her aunt had received them during her own coming-of-age ceremony and considered them sacred.

As Crystal held the slender branches in her hand, she honestly wondered how she'd ever be able to stir anything with them. With a long sigh, she set them aside carefully. Sitting cross-legged on the bed, she decided to practice sewing corn husks. Though the needle had no problem passing through the thin yellow-green husks, it was hard to keep from tearing them with the string she was using.

Finally, too weary to concentrate anymore, Crystal got ready for bed. She was sure that by teaming up with Junior she'd find her rug tomorrow, or at least discover who had it. Junior and she rarely thought alike, and that would be their greatest strength. Two heads were always better than one.

Chapter Seven

CRYSTAL WAS up before daybreak on Wednesday. Slipping into a pair of clean but well-worn jeans and a sweatshirt, she hurried into the kitchen. Within a few minutes she'd fixed her father's breakfast, covered it with another plate to keep it warm, and managed to wolf down a tortilla smeared with peanut butter. Grabbing her book bag, she charged out the back door. Early mornings in the desert were cold, so she broke into a run just to stay warm.

As the golden beams of sunlight struck the top of the Chuska Mountains far to the west, the certain knowledge that daylight would soon warm her and the desert filled her with a sense of purpose and order. Just knowing that some things were meant to be, renewed her sense of determination.

Junior and she *would* find the rug today. As she ran along the uneven path, streamers of light began to filter through the piñon pines, leaving paired needle patterns upon the rocks she passed. She took a big gulp of fragrant air, enjoying the exercise and the refreshing scent of pine pitch. She loved morning runs more than anything—except maybe weaving.

When she finally arrived at the halfway point between her home and Junior's, she looked around for him, but he was nowhere to be seen. Knowing he was as dependable as the sun and that he'd be there soon, she walked around for a few minutes to cool down, then sat down on a flat slab of sandstone to wait.

Her back to the sun and her arms wrapped around her knees, she pulled her legs up against her for warmth. Before long, she heard soft running footsteps she recognized as Junior's coming up the trail. He was so light-footed he barely left a footprint.

She stood up and waved as he came into view. He joined her seconds later.

"Are you ready?" he asked, scarcely winded though he'd been running at a strong pace.

"The way you cover ground you should join us on the cross-country team," she said.

He shook his head. "I don't have the time to go out for sports. School and learning to be a *hataalii* are all I can handle right now."

"You need to have fun too, you know—balance and all that."

He smiled. "And since when do you worry about balance and harmony?"

"Mostly when it applies to you and helps me win my argument," she answered with a grin.

"Are you ready to pay Biggins a visit?" he asked.

"Yeah," she said and grew serious again. "But I've been thinking about that, and I'm not sure you should come along."

"We're going together," he said firmly.

Crystal gave him a long look. His placid expression was deceptive. She'd known that for years. When Junior set his mind on something, there was no turning back.

"I sure wish you weren't so stubborn." Crystal sighed. "All right, if you insist, let's get started."

Muttering under his breath, he jogged effortlessly alongside her.

"We have a full day today, but only a half-day of school Thursday. Classes end at eleven, and then for lunch we'll all meet outside for the Culture Day cookout. Then, Friday, we're off the whole day—teachers' meeting. That's going to give us plenty of time to talk to people as well as do some more looking around before your ceremony on Saturday," he said.

"We'll have to stay alert and try to pick up clues without giving ourselves away."

By the time they were within sight of Biggins's house, the eastern sun gleamed in a cloudless blue morning sky. The ground haze that had settled late at night was already dissipating, so there wouldn't be much of anything to hide their approach. As they drew near the crest of a small hill adjacent to Biggins's home, they heard a horse whinnying and the stuttering bleats of goats.

Crystal and Junior dropped down into an arroyo that cut through a gap in the hill, then walked along the bottom, keeping watch on the house to their right, less than a hundred feet away. The sound of her breathing echoed slightly in the narrow canyon, and realizing it, Crystal made an effort to quiet down. As she glanced over at Junior, she couldn't help but notice—with a degree of annoyance—that Junior's breathing was as even as if he'd just had a leisurely stroll.

"There he is," Junior whispered, "by the corral. He's feeding the horses. And it looks like he's got a cast around his wrist."

"Where? I can't see him," Crystal said, stretching up to see over the side of the arroyo.

Junior pulled her down. "Down! We're not that far away."

"He doesn't know we're here. We have the advantage," she whispered back.

"Not for long, if you keep popping up like a duck in a shooting gallery."

Biggins finished feeding the horses, then gripping an ax halfway down the handle with one hand, began chopping wood.

"If he can do *that* with one hand, he could have dismantled my loom and taken the rug," she said.

"Where would he have hidden it?" Junior whispered, peering over the rim of the arroyo.

"I don't think he'd keep it in the house. I know his mom is really strict, and it would be tough for him to explain where, how, and why he got that rug," Crystal said. "So it must be in the barn or outside somewhere. He couldn't hide it in the pickup, I don't think. I'm going in for a closer look."

He grabbed her sleeve. "Are you nuts? To get any closer you'll have to step right out into the open. And let me remind you that you move as quietly as a herd of horses."

"I do *not*."

"Trust me. Stealth isn't one of your gifts."

"You're wrong and I'll prove it." Before he could react, she set down her book bag, then climbed out of the arroyo and crept toward the house, watching Biggins, who still had his back to her.

Crystal moved along the wooden fence, crouching low and hoping the slender logs would conceal her motion. With luck, the slight breeze and the thud of Biggins's ax would drown out the sound of her footsteps.

She was about fifty feet away from the old stump Biggins was using as a chopping block when she felt the sensation of movement behind her. Crouched low, she turned her head, and saw Junior only a few steps behind her. He pointed Navajo style by pursing his lips and gesturing toward Biggins. The big seventeen-year-old was muttering something as he chopped wood.

"Small-Man," he said, raising his ax. Then as it came down and split the piñon log neatly down the center, he added, "Now smaller."

Biggins picked up another piece of wood, then sliced it in half with one fluid stroke, the ax sinking into the stump with a thud. "Few-Feathers."

Realizing the danger, they knew they had to move quickly. Crystal cocked her head toward Biggins's truck. "The pickup—we need to check the tracks. Also we have to see if it has a trailer hitch and if there's a trailer around anywhere."

Junior held up his hand. "We can't go now—not while he's right there in the middle of the yard. But I've got an idea."

Junior raised one hand to his mouth, then suddenly there was a loud squeal from behind the storage shed. It sounded like two cats fighting.

Startled, Biggins jumped, missing the log he was swinging at and sticking the ax deep into the stump. Crystal and Junior dropped down low as he looked around curiously. Leaving the ax wedged in the stump, Biggins jogged around the corner of the shed to check things out.

"Was that you?" Crystal looked at him curiously.

Junior nodded. "I'm learning to throw my voice. But let's move. Check the truck's tires and back bumper. I'll look for a horse trailer."

Crystal sprinted to the pickup, peeked inside the cab and in the bed, then crouched down beside the rear wheel well. The pickup's tires left tracks that looked like the ones they'd seen at her place. But when she checked the back bumper, there was no trailer hitch.

Crystal was looking around, trying to figure out where a horse trailer could be parked, when she suddenly heard footsteps approaching. Peering out from behind the pickup, she saw that Biggins was only about thirty feet away.

Crystal's mouth went dry and her heart began to drum against her ribs. Fighting a surge of sheer panic, she looked around frantically for Junior. A breath later she spotted him as he looked over the rim of the arroyo, rose slightly, and threw a rock into the air. The rock arched across the sky and struck the metal roof of the house, which was farther away in the opposite direction. There was a loud clatter.

"Hey," Biggins yelled, then ran toward the house.

Seeing her chance, Crystal took off in the opposite direction, running at full speed for the arroyo. Junior waved her on silently and she jumped straight down, landing at a crouch on the sandy bottom. By then he'd already retrieved their book bags and moved down the arroyo, but she quickly matched his speed. Once they were behind the hill again, they climbed out and slowed down to a jog.

"That was too close, Birdie," he said, handing Crystal her book bag as they headed toward the trading post.

"Biggins came back around the shed faster than I thought he would," she said, finally slowing to a walk as they reached the trail Junior usually took to the bus stop.

"You were too busy looking around to keep an eye on him. Sometimes you get so fixed on one thing—like when you're weaving—that you develop severe tunnel vision. You wouldn't notice it if a bear came up behind you. And Biggins is worse than a bear right now. We could have found ourselves in a world of pain if he'd spotted us."

"I still could have outrun him—just like I can outrun you!"

She took off before he had a chance to react, and raced him to the bus stop at Hudson's.

She was waiting for him there when he arrived a few seconds later. She started to tease him about being a slowpoke, but suddenly realized that his cheeks weren't even flushed. "You weren't really trying!"

"I can't win no matter how I answer that, so I'm not going to say a word."

Crystal scowled at him and wondered why boys were so hard to figure out sometimes.

"I didn't see any signs of a horse trailer or a rug in the shed," Junior said. "What did you find?"

"The pickup tracks could have been a match, but there was no hitch on the truck, and I didn't see any sign of a trailer. There was no rug in the truck either."

"He could have been working with someone else," Junior suggested. "Let's see what else we can learn at school today, then afterward we can compare notes."

Crystal nodded, disappointed that she was no closer to finding the rug than she'd been last night. But there was no way she was going to let herself give up. One way or another she intended to find her rug.

A few moments later, the bus arrived and they climbed aboard. Mr. Anderson greeted them with a smile. "Hi kids!" He waited until they were seated, then put the bus in motion again. "If either of you hears of anyone who needs a handyman on weekends, let me know, okay?" he asked, glancing up at them in the big rearview mirror. "I'm looking around for some evening or part-time work. But don't spread it around. The school board doesn't like their employees to moonlight."

"Sure, Mr. Anderson," Crystal said. Everyone on the rez always needed money. But jobs, especially those that paid well, were scarce here. Feeling Junior watching her, she turned to look at him. "What?"

"Nothing," he said.

"Then why were you looking at me like that?"

"Looking at you like how?"

"I don't know—weird."

"What do you expect? You weird me out sometimes," he grumbled. "You're at the top of the game when it comes to weaving, Birdie. You've got that touch that comes along only once in a lifetime. It's something that could someday give you a real place of honor among our tribe. But then you go and do a dumb thing like—"

She jabbed him in the ribs with her elbow. "Sh-h-h! You can't tell *anyone*!" she whispered.

"Yeah, you're right," he answered, rubbing the spot on his side and grimacing. "I apologize for interfering with your business. But, Birdie, I'm worried about you, and I still can't figure out why you keep doing stuff you *know* will get you into trouble."

They didn't speak to each other for the rest of the trip to school. As they got off the bus, Lucinda and Holly came up to meet them. Crystal waved good-bye to Junior and walked off with her girlfriends.

This morning Holly seemed depressed, and the bags under her eyes showed that she hadn't slept well at all. "What's up? Are you coming down with something?" Crystal asked.

Holly shook her head, and Lucinda gave Crystal a worried glance.

"Hey, it's okay. We're friends. You can talk to us," Crystal said quietly.

"It's just that I still haven't been able to scrape up enough money to get my varsity cheerleading sweater, and if I don't have it for the next game, I'll have to sit in the bleachers. Without the right uniform it's just a matter of time before I'm asked to leave the squad."

"Is the sweater expensive?" Lucinda asked.

"Yeah," she said softly. "But before school even started, my parents cut up all their credit cards because we owed too much money. Now Mom says there's no way we can come up with the cash this month. I'm thinking of quitting the squad—it's better than getting kicked off."

"Did you ask your dad? Sometimes that works," Crystal said, then remembered that Mr. Anderson was looking for part-time work.

Holly shook her head. "I can't. He's still trying to get enough money together to pay for my brother Mike's college tuition second semester. My parents said they'd cover Mike's expenses his freshman year, but Dad hasn't been able to come up with the entire amount yet, so now he's trying to find some way to earn extra money. Mom told me not to even mention the sweater to Dad."

"What are you going to do?" Lucinda asked.

"I don't know. It's not like I can go right out and get a job. There aren't any for kids our age around here, and I don't have a way into town even if my parents would let me go. It just isn't fair. I worked so hard to make cheerleader!" Holly's shoulders slumped. "I guess I better start hoping for a miracle."

As Holly walked off to join two other cheerleaders who were talking beside the basketball court, Lucinda looked over at Crystal. "You normally have fifty thousand ways to get around a problem, cousin. How come you didn't come up with any ideas for Holly?"

Crystal exhaled softly. "I've got problems of my own now, and I guess I'm focused on that." She looked at Lucinda. "You know that rug I've been working on?"

"Sure." She suddenly smiled brightly. "Hey, do you think you can loan Holly the money she needs after you sell it?"

"First I'll have to get it back. Someone stole the rug yesterday while nobody was home," Crystal said, hoping to enlist her cousin's help.

Lucinda's eyes widened. "Someone *stole* your rug? Had you finished it?"

"No, but that didn't stop the thief. He, or she, slipped it off my loom," Crystal said, telling her the details. "But I'm going to find out who did it and get my rug back. Can you help me by keeping your ears open?"

"Sure I can. Maybe I can also find out which families have horse trailers."

"That'll be great. But, cousin, you can't tell anyone that my rug's been stolen. If it's still around and the thief thinks I'm bringing in the police, he'll just get rid of it. I've got to make him think I haven't reported it for some reason of my own. Maybe he'll get careless and give himself away. It's the best shot I've got."

As the bell rang, everyone headed into the building. Once inside, Crystal walked alone to her locker, wishing she could have confided more to her other friends. But clearly that was impossible. She couldn't tell Lucinda about the problem she was having every time she tried to weave, or that Junior thought it was Blanket Sickness. Any Navajo was bound to resent what she'd done by leaving out the spirit line. And the Anglos, like Holly, wouldn't understand at all.

Crystal went through her first two classes pretending to listen but not really concentrating on what the teachers were saying. Today, her attention was focused solely on the other kids. But her hopes that someone would soon drop a hint about her rug were dashed. By midmorning she'd found out absolutely nothing.

Her next class was P.E. Crystal headed for the locker room. As she suited up, she noticed that the kids she usually talked to seemed to be avoiding her. Once she got ready, Crystal walked into the gym. As soon as she did, Despah Joe, Vernon Joe's sister, came toward her and stopped, blocking her way. "You really are a jinx, Manyfeathers," she said, loud enough for everyone to hear. "Thanks to you we'll probably lose district. My brother and Biggins could have put the season away if it hadn't been for you. How we going to beat the Broncos now? Put you in *their* cafeteria?"

Crystal looked her straight in the eye, paying no attention to the other girls, who were starting to form a loose circle around her and Despah. "That was an accident and you know it. It never would have happened in the first place if Biggins hadn't been such a . . . pig!"

"Okay, track star. You want to get in my face, or you planning on running away?" Despah doubled up her fists and took another step toward Crystal, who held her ground. Then Mrs. Miller, their P.E. teacher, came into the gym from the opposite direction.

Mrs. Miller, a muscular blonde who looked like a professional weight lifter, recognized immediately what was going on and pushed her way past the group of girls. "It ends here and now, ladies. Whatever is going on is history. Now line up for roll call." She blew her whistle and everyone formed a line down the bleachers in alphabetical order, as usual, standing on numbers painted on the floor.

Today the evens played the odds in volleyball, and when Crystal's team took their side of the net, the girl selected as their team captain assigned positions. Crystal, though she was one of the best volleyball players, was left over. The way things were going today, she wasn't surprised.

"Everybody plays today," Mrs. Miller yelled, waving Crystal and the other team onto the court. With all the positions occupied, Crystal didn't know where to stand, so she walked toward the net.

Mrs. Miller threw her the ball. "No, Crystal. Serve instead."

Crystal ran to the server's position. The girl there gave her a snotty look, then walked to take a position by the net. "Any day, ladies," Mrs. Miller yelled, then blew her whistle. "Serve, Crystal."

Crystal dribbled the ball a few times, then held it in her palm and hit it hard with the end of her fist. The ball brushed the top of the net, hitting the floor before two lunging opponents could lay a hand on it.

"Net. Second serve, Crystal," Mrs. Miller yelled.

The ball was thrown back at her, hard, by Despah, but Crystal caught it without a word.

"Lucky catch," Despah snickered.

Angry, Crystal whacked the ball with everything she had. It struck the net right in front of Despah, who flinched.

Mrs. Miller blew her whistle. "Crystal, cool down. Take a seat on the bleachers. Despah, take a lap—outside!"

Despah grumbled, then walked toward the door. The track outside was a quarter-mile oval, and assigning a lap was Mrs. Miller's way of disciplining troublemakers.

Although it might have appeared that she was getting off easy, Crystal knew the coach was angry at her, too. Otherwise, she would have been the one taking a lap instead of Despah. Crystal loved to run and everyone knew it.

Crystal rested her elbows on her knees and, with a sigh, watched the girls play. She had a feeling that today would turn out to be the longest day of her life.

Chapter Eight

THAT AFTERNOON the bus dropped Junior and Crystal off at the usual location. After the bus departed, Crystal glanced at Junior, hesitated, then looked away.

"What's on your mind?" he asked.

"I don't want to get you into trouble, but I could sure use your help. Will you go inside the trading post with me and keep Mr. Albert busy while I take a look around? You know why."

Junior regarded her for a long moment. His expression was serene but his eyes were alert. "All right," he said at last. "I'll talk to him about that saddle I've had my eye on."

"Thanks." Crystal knew as well as Junior did that his chances of buying something that expensive were slim. "Keep him talking until I come up beside you, okay?"

"Sure, it'll be easy. He knows how badly I want that saddle. Maybe I can sound him out and see if he'll let me work for him part-time on weekends until I can earn enough to buy it."

As soon as they went inside, Junior immediately got Mr. Albert's attention. Crystal followed them until they were actually looking at the saddle, then slipped away, pretending to be looking at some bridles and bits.

Once she was sure Mr. Albert's attention was focused on Junior, she began to inch farther away. At first Crystal made sure that he could see her out of the corner of his eye as she studied the different horse blankets, then she went to the wall where he had his weaving supplies on display.

After a while, apparently having decided to let her browse freely, Mr. Albert turned his back to her. Crystal slipped into the storeroom in the back of the trading post. There were ceiling-high wooden shelves filled with clothing and dry goods, but no rugs anywhere. A few large cardboard boxes were by the wall, flaps opened, so she peered inside, but they only contained rolls of fabric, mostly velveteen and calico.

Crystal wandered back into the front room and waved at Mr. Albert as she headed toward the door. Hoping that Junior wouldn't assume that she'd forgotten their signal, she stepped outside onto the wide wooden porch. She knew that Mr. Albert's home, a double-wide trailer house with a small wooden porch, was directly behind the trading post, and she wanted to take a look around there, too.

As she stepped off the porch and headed around the side of the building, she saw Mrs. Albert, a skinny, well-tanned woman with dyed reddish orange hair, hanging out laundry.

Crystal stepped behind a tall, old piñon pine and kept watch for a moment. The open screen door at the back of the mobile home hadn't been latched, and it swayed back and forth gently in the breeze. Waiting to make sure Mrs. Albert wasn't looking, Crystal tiptoed quickly over to the door and ducked inside.

The Alberts' small home was as cluttered as the trading post, but it was spotless. The kitchen shelves held collections of salt and pepper shakers and candle holders in all kinds of sizes and shapes. Each had been meticulously dusted and polished to a high shine.

A long, narrow table was covered with a pure white tablecloth, and in its center was a blue crystal vase with one tiny red silk daisy. Watercolor paintings depicting scenes on the reservation were hung all around the kitchen, but there was no rug on either the floor or the walls.

Aware that the floor creaked slightly with each

step, Crystal stepped as lightly as possible as she went from room to room, peeking out the windows every few minutes to check on Mrs. Albert's progress with the laundry.

By the time Mrs. Albert had hung out all but the last few items, Crystal was ready to go. She hurried to the back door, but as she reached the kitchen, the phone suddenly rang. Crystal froze, her heart drumming in her ears. Gathering her wits, she rushed to the door, but before she could slip outside, she heard the light tapping of running footsteps coming toward the house.

With a gasp, Crystal ran to the living room and ducked behind the narrow partition behind the sofa that screened the living room from the hall. Seconds stretched out into eternities as she heard Mrs. Albert come in, pick up the phone, and begin talking to her friend. Crystal's heart was pounding so loudly she was sure Mrs. Albert would put the phone down and come searching for the booming noise.

By the time Mrs. Albert finally hung up, Crystal's entire body was covered in perspiration. Unless Mrs. Albert left the kitchen, Crystal would never be able to go back outside unnoticed.

Crystal thought about Junior. She had no idea

what he was doing now, but he was undoubtedly growing very worried about her and scrambling to keep Mr. Albert talking.

Then Mrs. Albert came into the living room and sat down on the sofa. Crystal scarcely breathed as she frantically tried to think of what to say if Mrs. Albert found her. Every excuse she could come up with to explain what she was doing there sounded lame, and Crystal knew it.

When Crystal heard Mrs. Albert stretch out on the couch, her stomach did a hard flip-flop, and for a few seconds, she was sure she'd be sick. Then Mrs. Albert sighed, grumbled something about the laundry, stood, and walked back out the kitchen door.

Shaking, Crystal bolted to her feet. Taking a quick look out the back door to verify that Mrs. Albert wasn't watching, she ducked out of the house. Crystal used the building to block herself from view as she hurried around the side of the house and ran down the road a few hundred yards. Once she was far enough away, she walked quickly back to the trading post.

Sitting down on the edge of the porch, she tried to catch her breath, sure that she was having her first heart attack. Before she could get herself together, Junior came out of the store and walked over to where she was. "Where have you been?" he asked in a harsh whisper.

"I'll tell you on the way home," she said quietly, standing up again.

Crystal told him everything as they walked. Finally she fell silent, but he didn't comment. Crystal, who'd always believed that there *was* such a thing as too much quiet, looked up at him. "Well, *say* something, even if it's an insult!"

"By going into their home uninvited, you've wronged them," he said in a heavy voice. "You stole their privacy."

"I could have been arrested and lost my reputation completely, and that's all you've got to say?" Crystal stared at him for several moments as they continued walking, then finally sighed. "Yeah, okay, you're right. And I do feel guilty, particularly now that I know they didn't steal my rug."

"You have to make it up to them somehow, Birdie. You have to restore the balance."

"If you think I'm going back there to tell them that I took an unguided tour of their house, you've lost your mind," she said flatly. "I did the wrong thing, but for the right reason."

"You don't have to confess, but maybe you can sell them a rug below cost in the future, or buy a few extra things at their store with the money you get when Mr. Albert sells your rug."

"I don't know if I believe in the need for balance—not in the sense you do—but I do feel bad about it. Since making it up to them is the only way I'm going to stop feeling this way, I'll do it."

"Have you found turquoise and white shell chips for the offering you'll be making to Spider Woman and Beautiful Flowers?" Junior asked.

She nodded and reached into her pocket. "I've got two tiny ones. They were given to me by my mom a long time ago."

"Then don't use those. They hold memories for you and you should keep them." He reached into his medicine pouch and retrieved a chip of turquoise and another of white shell. "Take these. They'll be good offerings. I picked them up during trips I took with Dad."

She took the fragments from his hand and studied them. The turquoise chip had a spiderweb marking in its center. "This would be perfect for Spider Woman," she said.

"I agree—that's why I chose it. And the shell has a pearly white sheen and would be great for Beautiful Flowers."

"I don't have to go home right away. Do you want to go to my family's shrine now?"

"Sure. How far is it?" he asked.

"It's a good forty-minute walk from my house, but we're not that far from the trail," she answered. "Less than an hour, probably."

"Let's get started then."

As they walked north, their path wound through narrowing canyons and ridges shaped by millions of years' worth of wind and water that had flowed from the heights above. The farther uphill they walked, the coarser the ground became, with most of the lighter material already eroded into the lower valleys and outwash plains. Boulders were taller here and the trees were more abundant.

Crystal glanced over at Junior after they'd been hiking silently for a half hour. "Where did you get the chips? They're really pretty for something so small."

"If I told you everything it would leave me bare and that dishonors knowledge."

"Which is a great way of saying you're not telling me, right?"

He nodded and smiled, stopping to catch his breath. "Do you know any Good Luck Songs? You should really sing one when you make the offerings."

Crystal nodded. "I know a personal song my mom made up. She said I was to guard and keep it secret, that it was something between our family and the gods."

Junior nodded. "We all have songs that stay within our clan."

She paused, then with a smile added, "But since you gave me the chips, I'll share the song with you."

He nodded in approval. "Balance."

As they continued, Crystal found herself wishing that her family's shrine had been in a more public place—maybe with a nearby road so people driving by would see them. She needed word to reach the person who'd taken her rug in case it was just someone out to punish her.

"Tell me about your family's shrine," Junior said.

Crystal noted that, like her, he was watching where he placed his feet. The terrain had become a lot steeper now, and there were many rocks that could conceal rattlesnakes.

She told him what she knew about the shrine. "It's a place of good luck for our clan. We all visit it whenever we're facing a problem."

By the time they arrived at the small grottolike opening in the sandstone cliff, both were winded and tired. The climb had been hard, especially the last few hundred feet, and the footing treacherous since the late-summer rains had washed away much of the trail.

Crystal pointed to the mound of rocks placed carefully against the rear of the cave. "That's the cairn I was talking about," she said.

Tiny pieces of white shell gleamed from the shallow cavity in the flat rocks at the top of the cairn. As they drew near they could see small pieces of hard coal, turquoise, and a rainbow of pastels swirling within a chip of silver-tinged abalone.

"The four sacred stones are all there," Junior muttered with a nod.

Beside the cairn, on the sandy floor of the cave, Crystal noticed a prayer stick, a special offering to the gods. It was made of wood painted blue, pink, and black, and wrapped in a corn husk. "My dad must have been here recently," she said. "I recognize his work."

As she stared at the prayer stick, she felt a lump form in her throat. There'd been a time when they'd only come here as a family. "This place has a lot of memories for me," she said, aware that Junior was watching her.

"I know," he said softly. "But don't think of the past right now. We have other work to do."

Crystal took the chips he'd given her out of her jacket pocket. Then, placing the turquoise on the top of the cairn, she cleared her throat and, in a soft voice, began her Good Luck Song calling for everlasting blessings and peace. Her voice was perfectly pitched, rising strongly, then softening as she'd been taught.

Maybe part of it was due to the amplifying effect of the small stone chamber she was standing in, but as she sang, she could feel the song's power. It affirmed each person's place within the circle of life and made her feel warm inside despite the cool bite of the air at this altitude.

After she sang the last note, she turned to Junior and saw the amazed look on his face. "You've never heard me sing because I've always been too shy around other people," she said hesitantly. "Did you think I sounded like an old bullfrog?"

"No, not at all. Your song was . . . well, beautiful."

She smiled. "It was the song, not me. My mom had many of these, and when she sang even the birds became quiet so they could listen to her."

"It was that way for you too, just now."

"No, not quite," she said with a shy smile. "The birds probably flew away to escape the racket, and that's what threw you."

He laughed, then caught himself and grew serious once more. "Now we need to find a beautiful open flower with strong petals. If the white shell drops to the ground before I sing my Good Medicine Song, you'll attract bad luck."

"I'm already a magnet for bad luck. I can't afford any more, so we'd better do this right."

They started walking downhill, searching the steep slopes immediately around them for a suitable flower, but they weren't able to find any that were quite right. As they climbed farther down the cliff, Crystal grew impatient. "Maybe we don't have to look for a sturdy flower. I've got a glue stick in my backpack. With a little stickum I can make sure the stone stays exactly where it should be."

He stopped searching and glowered at her. "Do you really want to be able to weave again? Ever?"

She clamped her mouth shut and kept on searching. At long last, Crystal found a small Rocky Mountain bee plant in a tiny arroyo leading away from the slope. The pinkish multi-petaled flower was healthy, and the petals were clustered together tightly. "I think this flower would hold the white shell."

Crystal crouched down and, with her face inches from the flower, slid the small shell among the petals. But before she could move away, her nose began to tickle, and a powerful urge to sneeze swept over her.

"Oh, no." She moved back quickly but, unable to suppress it any longer, sneezed loudly.

Junior gasped as the little flower moved back and forth. But, as if held by an unseen hand, the stone remained exactly where she'd placed it.

"I can't believe you sneezed!" Junior said.

"I couldn't help it! But the shell is still there."

Junior stood straight, then began singing the song his father had taught him. His voice rose commandingly, calling down blessings. Crystal was sure that the rich melody would compel the gods to listen.

When at last they headed back, they remained silent for quite a while. The trip, mostly downhill, was a lot easier. Finally Crystal spoke. "As soon as I get back home, I'm going to give weaving a try again."

"It's too soon for that. You shouldn't even try to weave anything new until you fix what you did and put a spirit line in your rug—assuming we can get it back."

"You don't think that the gods will still punish me now, do you? I can't fix a rug that's *missing*. If they really want me to add the spirit line, then they're going to have to help me get it back."

"*You're* responsible for the mess you're in, not the gods. You started this when you deliberately ignored your mom's teachings. You knew precisely what you were doing, Birdie."

She sighed, realizing that what he'd just said was the truth. "Life is so complicated. I'm always feeling torn between what I want to be and what I am."

"You can't be who you want to be unless you honor who you already are."

Crystal remained quiet, considering what Junior had said, as they headed back home.

When they finally reached the crossroads that would lead them in different directions, she looked up at him. "No matter how we look at this problem, the key is finding my rug. I'm through keeping my ears open, hoping someone will confess or slip up and say too much. Tomorrow I'll ask everyone I see—students and staff—if they've heard anything about a thief operating in this area. Maybe I can uncover something that way."

"Just don't tip your hand and let others know what happened to your rug."

"Don't worry, I'll be careful. But I've got to do *something,* and this is the only thing I can think of doing right now."

Chapter Nine

THURSDAY MORNING, Crystal was sitting on the brick planter that bordered the front of the school building, waiting for the bell, when Holly ran up to her.

She was so happy she was almost bouncing up and down. "I've got great news, Crystal! I was able to order my cheerleading sweater, and I'll have it in time for the next game!"

"That's outstanding! How did you get the money?" Crystal lowered her voice. "Did your father manage to find some handyman work?"

Holly shook her head. "No, I did this on my own. Well . . . almost. I just kept at it until I found a way."

"Hey, you're not supposed to hold back on your friends! 'Fess up. How did you do it?"

"It's a crazy story, and there's not enough time to tell it now," she said, then waved at two other cheerleaders across the ground, beside the gym entrance. “I’ve got to go tell Raynell and Martha. I’ll talk to you later in class, okay?”

As Holly ran off, Crystal’s mind began working furiously. She hated to think badly of her friend, but knowing how desperate Holly had been the other day, she just couldn’t help but wonder. . . .

“Hey, you’re off all by yourself this morning!” Lucinda said cheerfully, walking over and taking a seat beside Crystal. “What’s up?”

Crystal told her about Holly’s sweater. “I hate that I’m even thinking this, but I know her parents are really short of money right now. . . .”

“You know who your friends are, girl. And Holly’s one of the best. She wouldn’t steal from anyone. She even gives back pencils—really.”

“I know she’s always been perfectly honest, but she really did want that sweater, and yesterday she was almost in tears,” Crystal said, then shook her head. “No, you’re right. I’m being stupid and unfair. Holly wouldn’t do that to me. I think this whole thing on top of the *Kinaaldá* is making me nuts.”

“I know. The time right before the ceremony is the worst—but it’s worth it in the end, Crystal. You’ll see. The *Kinaaldá* changes you.” She saw Crystal’s skeptical look and quickly added, “It does. You wait. And you’ll never forget it.”

"I may just drop dead from exhaustion," she muttered.

"You won't, you dummy. The excitement alone will keep you going. And when it's over you're going to feel really special."

"Maybe it's just endorphins from all that running," Crystal said.

"You're impossible, cuz," Lucinda said. "You always want things to be as clear and simple as equations are to you in math class. But except for your gift for weaving we're really not that different from each other. That's why I can tell you that, even though you can't see it now, you're really going to be glad you went through the ceremony."

"But I can't just accept things as easily as you can. I need to understand the whys and hows. And I don't see anything wrong with that."

Junior, who'd come up while they were talking, glanced at Lucinda, and when she nodded, he answered, "It's wrong because what you're really doing is trying to ignore what you are."

"I'm just not happy following the ways you love," Crystal said, giving Junior a weak smile. "But I'm glad we can be different from each other and still be friends."

"You *need* to have a friend like me," he said.

Then, in a barely audible voice, he added, "You may not know who you are and will be, but *I* do."

Suddenly the bell rang, and they were forced to hurry inside. Crystal wasn't able to ask Junior what he meant, but there was no way she was going to forget that cryptic remark.

These past few months, Junior's attitude toward her had changed. Lately she'd had the strangest feeling that he was waiting for her to do or say something, though she had no idea what.

Every once in a while, she'd catch him looking at her oddly, or he'd say something cryptic, as he had this morning. She was sure he was keeping something from her that concerned her in a very real and tangible way.

As she struggled silently to find an answer, Crystal suddenly remembered the many times she'd overheard her mom and dad talking about her in whispers. The minute they'd see her, they'd invariably change the subject. She couldn't help but wonder if the past and present were connected somehow.

Crystal went through her morning classes talking, whenever she got the chance, in general terms about thefts on the rez. If one of the kids had taken her rug, hopefully, the person would do or say something to give himself away.

At eleven, regular classes stopped and Culture Day events began. Today, their school was hosting two speakers—a stargazer and an elderly *hataalii*—who'd be telling students about their very traditional Navajo professions. The event would be topped off by a mutton stew lunch prepared outside on the school grounds.

It was a golden opportunity for Crystal. With everyone gathered there at once and not having to worry about the restrictions of the classroom, she was hoping to get a lead that would help her find her rug.

Crystal headed down the main hall toward the soccer field at the back of the school, following a stream of other kids as their classes were dismissed. As she stepped outside, she saw that Culture Day was already in full force. A huge truck with the words WILKINSON'S TRADING POST had been parked behind some cooking equipment it had apparently brought, such as portable stoves and metal grills. Cafeteria staff and parent volunteers were doing the cooking, and her mouth watered as she caught a whiff of freshly cooked fry bread, corn on the cob being roasted over coals, and mutton stew heating in kettles the size of washtubs.

Junior came up to her. "It sure smells good, doesn't it? I'm glad that Wilkinson's Trading Post decided to sponsor the cookout. With money tight, I heard that the school had a big problem finding a sponsor."

"Isn't that your dad?" Crystal asked, gesturing to where Mrs. Todacheene was standing with a group of adults.

"Yeah. I was surprised to see him here. The *hataalii* originally scheduled had an emergency with a patient near Teece Nos Pos, so my dad was asked if he could substitute. He said yes, of course."

She heard the pride in Junior's voice and wasn't a bit surprised. Junior thought the world of his dad. Part of the reason he wanted to be a *hataalii* was because he respected his father so much.

Crystal was certain that Junior would be a great *hataalii* someday. He had the same presence Mr. Tallman had, easily capturing and holding everyone's attention when he spoke.

Kids began to gather around in a loose circle as Mrs. Todacheene introduced Mr. Tallman. Not using the microphone provided, he began his talk, moving back and forth purposefully.

"Aqalani," he said, using the Navajo word for greetings. "I'm here to tell you about being a *hataalii.*" He began by explaining the healing power of chants, then continued. "We have other ways to heal that we use along with our chants. War

Eagle taught us about sandpaintings. We make those so that the Holy People can enter through them and heal the person being sung over. Then, after the sandpainting absorbs the sickness, we destroy it—and the illness.

"*Hataaliis* also have to learn about plants," he continued. "The Holy People gave us the Plant People so that we could eat and have medicines. We use the gifts the Plant People bring us in many different ways during our ceremonies. Life Way medicines bring us health. Other herbs and plants not used for healing also play important roles in our ceremonies. But everything has to be done in a certain way, or the gods won't accept our prayers. For instance, in the Night Chant—our ceremony to cure blindness, deafness, and certain other ailments—one plant must be gathered only when lightning flashes. There's a lot for a *hataalii* to learn, and it can take us years," he said. He finished his presentation by detailing his many duties.

At long last he gestured proudly toward Junior. "Someday, my son will continue our traditions by also becoming a Singer for the tribe."

Junior, surprised, gave everyone a tentative smile, and Crystal suddenly realized that Junior felt he would never be able to fill his parent's shoes. For that one moment, she understood him completely.

She gave his hand a gentle squeeze and he jumped, but when he turned to look at her, he was smiling.

The stargazer, a very old, tiny, fragile-looking woman with white hair and a clear, high-pitched voice, spoke next. First she explained briefly about the Navajo tradition of stargazing. "A stargazer's talent is not based on knowledge, like the *hataalii*'s. It's a gift. When I hold a rock crystal and point it in the direction of a star, a vision will appear for me. Sometimes I can tell exactly what's wrong with a *hataalii*'s patient, other times I locate things people have lost. To enhance this ability, we make a special medicine that comes from the tears of the eagle." She pointed to the medicine bundle she kept attached to her belt. "We keep the medicine with us to help us help others," she said, then continued telling them about the many different experiences she'd had over the years.

After her talk ended, Junior couldn't wait to go up and meet her. Crystal went with him, curious to find out more. As tempted as she was to ask the stargazer to find her rug, Crystal knew she couldn't do that. She didn't have the money to hire her, and also she was reluctant to let anyone else in on her secret.

The stargazer appeared to be in her late eighties, yet her voice was strong and she walked upright and unaided. As they approached, the woman's sparkling black eyes fixed on Crystal, and she suddenly smiled.

"I knew I'd meet you here today," she said.

Crystal looked at the wrinkled old woman, careful not to look her straight in the eye, which was considered inappropriate. "I'm sorry, aunt, have we met before?" Crystal considered calling her "grandmother" because of their widely differing ages, but decided against it.

She laughed. "I'm not surprised you don't remember, child, you barely had your eyes open that day. I was there when you were born."

Junior's eyes widened. "Are *you* the stargazer I've been told can make predictions?"

"I rarely do that, nephew," she said, using the term not out of kinship, but to acknowledge him as younger, yet worthy of respect.

"But you can—and did?" he pressed.

She looked directly at him and nodded, her eyes narrowing mysteriously. "There have been rare occasions when I've gazed into my quartz stone and have seen . . . surprises." She looked at Crystal and smiled gently.

Crystal felt decidedly uncomfortable. She had the strangest feeling they were talking about her, though neither of them had been specific.

"Do you weave often?" the seer asked her.

Thinking that maybe her small pieces had already garnered some attention in the community, Crystal smiled. "I weave as often as I can. I love everything about it—from working with the wool itself to sitting in front of the loom."

"That is as it should be, then. But everything one does in life demands sacrifice and humility," the stargazer said somberly. "Remember that, niece."

For one crazy moment Crystal was sure the stargazer knew that she'd omitted the spirit line in her latest rug. A surge of panic shot through her and it took all the willpower she had to remain still. "I'll keep it in mind, aunt," she said.

"The more skills and talent a person has, the more will be expected of them. It's the way of life," the seer added.

When another student came up to talk to the stargazer, Crystal took the opportunity to slip away, and Junior followed.

As soon as they were out of earshot, Crystal turned to look at Junior. "Tell me something. Am I crazy, or were you two talking about me?"

"To answer your first question—yes, you're crazy. Which, come to think of it, answers your second question too."

Crystal scowled. "I had the funniest feeling when you were talking to her— "

"Did you *listen* to her advice?" he challenged, interrupting her.

"I heard what she said. For a second there I even thought she knew that my rug didn't have a spirit line."

"She's one of the most respected stargazers our tribe has. My dad works with her often. You really should be honored that she was there when you were born. A lot of women practically beg her to come and attend their children's births. The seer's presence is considered good luck. But she seldom goes, so she must have known your mother pretty well."

Crystal shrugged helplessly. "I could ask my dad."

"Just remember her advice, Birdie. She doesn't give it often."

"You *do* know something that you're not telling me, don't you?" Her eyes narrowed as she studied his expression. "What's going on? Am I adopted or something?" Then she remembered how much she looked like her mother. "Scratch that question. But what's going on?"

"If I were keeping a secret, then I couldn't tell you about it, could I? But I will promise that you'll know everything you need to at exactly the right time—not before and not afterward."

"I knew it! There *is* something you're holding back! Is it something to do with my *Kinaaldá*?" When he didn't answer, she added, "Why won't you tell me? I won't tell anyone you told me."

"I've always been a good friend to you, Birdie. You know that. I don't know anything about you that you don't already know."

"What does that mean?"

"Do you believe I'm your friend?" Seeing her nod, he added, "Then trust me. I've always been on your side."

He *was* her best friend. He wouldn't have kept anything from her that she absolutely needed to know, even if it had been a closely guarded secret.

"I think you should focus on getting your rug back and fixing things before the *Kinaaldá* this weekend," he said. "That's what's most important now."

"I've been on the trail of my rug." Crystal told him about Holly and her sweater. "I know she wouldn't steal, and neither would her parents, but I still can't get that coincidence out of my mind."

He remained quiet for several moments, then, almost reluctantly, said, "Did you know that Holly's second-oldest brother, Ray, was arrested a few months ago for shoplifting? His parents squared it with the shop owner because they didn't want Ray to face charges."

"I didn't know *that*!" Crystal said. "I've got to go find Holly. See you later, Junior."

As Crystal wound her way through the crowd of students, most of whom were in groups talking and laughing as they waited for lunch, she heard her name. Mrs. Todacheene was speaking to a tall Anglo man wearing a baseball cap that said WILKINSON'S TRADING POST.

Curious, Crystal turned away so her face wasn't visible, then stood still and eavesdropped on the conversation.

"So you teach weaving here at school?" he asked.

"Yes, it's part of home economics. But Crystal has already gone far beyond what we're able to cover in class. She didn't learn to weave from us. Her mother, and her mother before that, going back as far as anyone can remember, were all very accomplished weavers. The girl was born with the talent, and her mother helped her develop it to the level you see now."

"I've seen only the smaller pieces she's woven,

but I've got to say they're very impressive. Someday I hope to buy some of her rugs so I can sell them at my trading post. Work like hers is getting to be a lost art, even here in the Navajo Nation."

"Crystal *is* very gifted. As I said, it's a family thing."

Crystal had never heard Mrs. Todacheene praise anyone to this degree before, and it surprised her. Maybe more people knew about her weaving skills than she realized. And Mr. Wilkinson's interest in her work was exciting. It opened new possibilities for her, though she knew she'd have to have her father negotiate the terms.

Her father didn't have a college degree, but he was an excellent businessman. The deal he'd made with Mr. Albert had been profitable for all. Mr. Albert paid an advance in order to show her work, then got a percentage commission, on consignment, rather than buying the piece wholesale and selling it at retail.

Lucinda spotted Crystal and waved. "Isn't this fun?" she said as she joined her. Noticing that Crystal was empty-handed, she held out her paper bowl. "This stew's great! The mutton is so tender it almost melts in your mouth. Taste," she said.

When Crystal tasted it, she suddenly realized

that she was starving. “I’d better get some food before it’s all gone.”

Lucinda walked with her over to the line, which was dwindling now. “What were you doing over there, staring off into space, like you were actually thinking instead of goofing off like the rest of us?”

“I was eavesdropping on a conversation that man with the baseball cap was having with Mrs. Todacheene about me. He’s apparently interested in selling my rugs.”

“Well, sure he is. He’s Mr. Albert’s competitor. You’ve probably never been to Wilkinson’s Trading Post because you live so close to Hudson’s. I hear Wilkinson’s isn’t doing well. I’m not really sure what the deal is, but more and more Navajos have stopped doing business with the store. My mother never goes there. She only buys from Mr. Albert.”

“I wonder why? I was thinking of having my dad work out a deal with him so he could sell my rugs too. But maybe I’d better find out more about him first.”

“By the way, I’ve been asking around to see who has a horse trailer, but most of the families here don’t have one. If the horse needs to go to the vet’s, either the doctor comes over or the horse is walked there. But I hear Mr. Wilkinson has a trailer that he rents out.”

"I need to find out if anyone rented his horse trailer the day before yesterday when my rug was taken."

"That could be tricky. How are you going to ask a question like that?"

"I don't know. Maybe Junior and I can find a way to sneak a peek at his rental records," she said, remembering how they'd teamed up at Mr. Albert's.

They reached the front of the food line moments later—Lucinda for seconds and Crystal for her first serving. Taking a generous portion, Crystal left the line and sat down on the ground as many others had already done, and began to eat.

Lucinda watched the crowd as she munched on a piece of fry bread. "There's Holly, hanging out with the other cheerleaders. She sure is happy they won't have to ask her to leave the squad now."

Crystal, whose mouth was full, simply nodded. Swallowing at last, she looked at Lucinda and asked, "Where's Ray? Is he still around?"

"Last time I saw him he was over by the basketball court with some other seniors, I think. Do you need to talk to him?"

Crystal shrugged. "Nah, I'm just curious about him."

Lucinda's eyes widened. "Don't tell me you like him! I thought you and Junior—"

"No, I don't *like* Ray, not in the way you mean," she said quickly. "I barely even know him. But something Junior told me has stayed on my mind." She told Lucinda what she'd learned about Ray's shoplifting charges.

"I hadn't heard about that. Holly never said a word to me."

"We really should keep it quiet for Holly's sake, and for her parents, who are good people. I only found out a few minutes ago when Junior told me."

"So now you want to know if he might have taken your rug, sold it, and then given part of the money to his sister?"

"Yeah," Crystal admitted. "I feel like a rat for even thinking of that possibility, but it does make sense, doesn't it?"

"Yeah, but—" Seeing Holly approaching, Lucinda glanced at Crystal and added, "We'd better change the subject."

Holly joined them, a big smile on her face. "I saw you with Junior," she said, her eyes sparkling as she looked at Crystal. "The way he looks at you really does say it all! He's got it bad."

"Are you crazy? Junior? I've known him all my life. He's my friend—that's all."

"Crystal, sometimes you just don't see what's right in front of you! But I saw it, and I can't be fooled."

Crystal rolled her eyes. “Honestly!”

Lucinda laughed. “Holly’s right, you know.”

“You think so too?”

Lucinda nodded. “Junior likes you. It’s right there on his face every time he looks at you.”

“You’re both crazy, and I don’t want to talk about this anymore,” Crystal said, suddenly feeling extremely awkward.

Holly laughed. “What shall we talk about, then?”

“How about your brother Ray?” Crystal blurted out.

Holly’s eyes grew wide. “*You* like my brother? Well, I don’t blame you one bit. He’s wonderful, but I warn you, he already has a girlfriend.”

Realizing that she couldn’t explain what was really on her mind now without hurting Holly’s feelings, Crystal looked away, trying to figure out what to say next. She’d brought the subject up in precisely the wrong way. Now she had no idea how to get the information she needed without letting Holly think she was interested in her brother.

“But don’t worry. It’s not hopeless or anything. He changes girlfriends often,” Holly said, misinterpreting her silence completely.

“Tell me something. Is it true that he once got arrested for shoplifting?”

“Yeah,” she said soberly. “Ray slipped up. He

saw something he really wanted, it cost more money than he had, so he took it. Of course, he got caught. Mom and Dad came down real hard on him, and I know he'll never do anything like that again. But sometimes it's hard not being able to afford things, you know?"

"What kind of things does he take?" Crystal asked.

Holly glared at her. "It's not like he's a professional thief," she said, then stopped and looked at her. "What is it, you want the excitement of hanging around a bad boy, and you think Ray's one?"

Crystal's mouth dropped. "I—" For a moment she couldn't think of a single thing to say.

Lucinda gave Crystal a quick look, then answered for her. "Crystal loves the older, dangerous guys."

"Well, that explains why you haven't fallen for Junior. He's as safe as they get."

"No, he's not. Maybe he seems that way sometimes, but he's really very mysterious," Crystal answered before she realized that it was precisely the wrong thing to say.

Holly's eyes narrowed. "So you *don't* want to hook up with my brother. What's really going on?"

"Nothing," Crystal said with a shrug. "I just wanted to know more about Ray."

"I've figured that out by now, but why?" She looked at Crystal, her eyes narrowing and her tone suspicious now. "Tell me the real reason you're interested in my brother."

"Don't be angry at her, Holly," Lucinda said. "It's just that someone's stolen the rug she just finished weaving."

Crystal glared at Lucinda. "That's supposed to be a secret," she said.

"And you think my brother stole it from you?" Holly's voice rose. "Is that it? What would he want with your dumb rug?"

"I didn't want to accuse Ray," Crystal answered. "I just wondered if—" suddenly an idea came to her— "if he knew what people do with stolen stuff around here. Is there anyone who's known to buy stuff like that, like a crooked art dealer or whatever?"

"Oh, I get it!" Holly sounded relieved, then she thought about the question for a moment before finally shaking her head. "I really don't know, and I doubt he would either." Seeing some of her other friends, Holly said a quick good-bye and wandered off.

"I'm still not really convinced that Ray's innocent," Crystal said as soon as they were alone. "He could have sold my rug, then given some of the money to Holly. It's not like he would have told her where he got the money. You can tell how she really looks up to him."

"That's true. I sure hope he doesn't have anything to do with what happened. That would break Holly's heart."

Crystal nodded, then took another spoonful of stew.

"I'm still hungry," Lucinda announced, staring into her empty bowl. "I'm going to see if there's any more. Want to come?"

"No, I'm not all that hungry right now. You go ahead."

As Lucinda walked off, Mr. Tallman, Junior's dad, approached Crystal.

"How are things going for you, niece?" he greeted her pleasantly.

"Just fine, uncle. We made the offering, just as you recommended," she said.

"Good," he said, "but that's only half of it."

"I know. Your son's already reminded me."

He smiled with pride when she mentioned Junior. "He's got a lot of sense already. You can trust him never to steer you wrong."

"I do trust him," Crystal said honestly, then with her usual directness, added, "but I think he's got a secret he's keeping from me, and that makes me nervous." She waited, hoping she'd get an answer or perhaps at least a clue from Junior's father, but when he didn't comment, she continued. "I got the impression a while ago that the stargazer knows as well—that it's a secret they both share. I'd sure love to find out what it is."

"You will, I'm sure," he said quietly. "But sometimes getting an answer from someone else isn't good enough. There are times when we need to work things out for ourselves."

As he walked away, Crystal stood there, biting back her frustration. Why were Junior and his father always so cryptic? Although what Mr. Tallman had said made sense, she could easily have argued that getting a quick answer had merits, too.

Chapter Ten

AS JUNIOR and Crystal got off the school bus, Mr. Albert came to the entrance of the trading post, almost as if he'd been waiting for them. "How did the cookout go?" he asked in a cheerful tone as he opened the screen door and stepped out onto the covered porch.

"It was great. The food was wonderful," Crystal said.

Mr. Albert nodded. "Was everyone satisfied with the way things turned out?"

"Yeah, I guess," Junior said.

Crystal knew that, as a Navajo, Junior carefully avoided speaking for another person, and Mr. Albert should have known that. But the trader seemed nervous today—unless it was just her overactive imagination acting up. Curious, she watched him carefully.

"What did Wilkinson do—I mean, besides provide the cooking equipment?" Mr. Albert asked.

"I'm not sure. All I know is that he was talking to Mrs. Todacheene for a while," Crystal said. It suddenly occurred to Crystal that Mr. Albert was trying to determine how much of a good impression his competitor had made at the school.

"The whole thing was just a public relations gimmick for him. He didn't do it to support public education," Mr. Albert said crossly.

"It still helped us out. I doubt the school would have had the cookout otherwise," Crystal said. "I also found out something exciting. Mr. Wilkinson knows about my weaving and is very impressed with my work."

"Ah, let me guess. He offered to buy your rugs so he can sell them in his store, right?"

"No, not quite. Actually I didn't even speak to him. I was just standing nearby and I happened to overhear bits of his conversation with Mrs. Todacheene."

"I've known you since before you could walk, Crystal, and I wouldn't steer you wrong. If you want to find other outlets for your work you can do a lot better than Wilkinson. Riley Smith, who has a shop in Farmington, is already interested in your work, and he has outlets all over the state. But stay away from that little shop in Waterflow."

"Thanks for letting me know, Mr. Albert. I appreciate it, really."

"Before I forget, remember that I'll need to have your rug here no later than Monday morning."

Crystal's stomach sank. "I know. I'll do my best."

Hearing the phone ring inside the store, Mr. Albert said a quick good-bye and stepped back inside.

As she tried to figure out what to do next, she remained quiet. Then at last she spoke. "Do you think it's possible that the thief took my rug to that place in Waterflow?" Crystal asked Junior.

"We should go check it out, but we need to get a ride. It's over forty miles from here."

"We'll have to figure out who to ask. In the meantime, why don't you come over? We can test things out and see what happens when I try to weave again."

They walked to Crystal's home, and, once there, she grabbed her tools and leftover yarn, then led the way outside to the loom.

Crystal shortened the height of her working area to make a small rug no larger than a place mat, then got off to an enthusiastic start. The first step requiring yarn was warping the loom, which looped yarn vertically around the top and bottom beams. The warps, laid out in pairs, had to be evenly spaced. After about a half hour, she felt her thoughts drifting as she worked, and although she fought to stay alert, it didn't work.

Before she knew it, Junior was shaking her awake. "Aw, rats!" she muttered. Crystal shook the cobwebs out of her mind and sat back to look at her work. The warp was totally uneven and would have to be completely redone.

"I told you that you couldn't take shortcuts. You have to restore the balance the hard way—by correcting what you did wrong. Until the rug has a spirit line, nothing will get back to normal for you."

Thoroughly discouraged, Crystal led the way inside to the kitchen. She reached into the refrigerator, got out some tomato juice, and poured each of them a glass.

A few minutes later, they heard the sound of a vehicle driving up the road. Crystal and Junior stepped outside and saw an old Ford pickup approaching.

Someone stuck her head out of the passenger's side window and waved. It wasn't hard to tell who it was because the second the sunlight touched Holly's red hair, it gleamed as if it were on fire. When the truck pulled to a stop in front of her home,

Crystal realized that Ray was driving, and Holly and Lucinda had crowded into the front with him.

Lucinda threw the door open and both girls ran toward the truck. When they reached Crystal, Holly smiled at Junior. “Excuse us, Junior. We need to borrow her for a moment,” she said, and taking Crystal’s arm, led her away.

Filled with curiosity, Crystal allowed herself to be led toward the empty corrals. “What’s going on?”

Holly glanced over at Lucinda, then smiled at Crystal. “Lucinda and I were talking about how crazy the missing rug’s been making you and we understand totally. If either of us had worked on something like that for almost forever like you did, we’d be going nuts too.”

“It really is hard,” Crystal admitted. “I was counting on wearing it for my *Kinaaldá*. And, to make everything even worse, I could miss my first major sale unless the rug turns up before Monday.”

“What are you going to do?” Lucinda asked.

“I’m not sure.”

Holly gave her a worried look. “Maybe you’re too close to this. What you need is to put it out of your mind for a little while. Come with us to Farmington. My sweater’s ready to be picked up at the store there.”

"I'd love to go," Crystal said. "Junior too?"

"Of course. You can both ride in the back, inside the camper shell. You'll be alone together." Holly looked over at Junior, who was watching them, and smiled. "It'll be romantic."

"Holly, only you would think that riding in the back of a pickup going over bumpy dirt roads is romantic," Crystal said. "Besides, how many times do I have to tell you—"

"I know, I know, you're only friends. But I don't believe you," she said with a happy grin.

They ran back over to where Junior was waiting, then piled into the truck. Ray, Holly, and Lucinda sat in front as before, and Junior and Crystal climbed into the back."You guys still okay back there?" Ray called out once they reached the highway after a bumpy, dusty two-mile drive.

"Yeah, sure," Junior said.

Lucinda opened the rear window of the cab so they could talk without shouting, now that the dust wasn't going to be a problem. "Hey, what do you say we all stop at the pizza place after we pick up Holly's sweater?"

Crystal gave Junior a quick look, then glanced back at Lucinda. "We're broke, but we'll sit with you guys, if you want, or go window-shopping."

"Don't worry about that. I've been working for

my mom in the afternoons and I've got enough to buy all of us a soft drink and maybe a few slices of pizza," Lucinda said.

"Hey, can you get *me* a job working for your mom?" Ray asked.

Lucinda shook her head. "Sorry, Ray. The only reason she hired me is because I work cheap. But I decided to keep setting my money aside in a shoe box, and it added up."

"I put whatever I make from weaving into the bank," Crystal explained. "Once I get ready to go to college, that money will be there waiting for me."

Holly looked back at Crystal. "I wish I were more like you. You always plan ahead so well. You already know where you're going and what you'll do once you graduate. I still don't have a clue."

"Neither do I," Lucinda admitted.

Ray glanced back at her in the rearview mirror. "You and I have something in common then, Crystal. I know what I want to do—leave home and make my own way."

"Are you thinking of college?" Crystal asked.

Ray nodded. "Yeah, eventually. My grades won't get me a scholarship, but I plan to join the army—the Rangers, if I can get in."

When Crystal glanced at Junior, she saw that he hadn't been impressed by Ray's comment. "Junior's going to be a medicine man, so he knows what's ahead for him too."

"Well, at least you won't have to go to college for that, right?" Ray asked.

"It's not required, but I will. I'll probably major in botany or something like that. Hopefully, I'll be as good a *hataalii* as my dad."

Ray glanced at Holly. "You and I are outgunned when we compare ourselves to those two," he said with a grin.

Holly nodded. "But it's not hopeless. I believe what our Sunday school teacher always says—that if we ask, God will make sure we make the right choices."

Ray rolled his eyes. "Naive kid. You believe everything you're told."

Holly looked back at Crystal. "My brother and you are a lot alike. He doesn't believe in anything he can't see or touch."

Ray glanced back in the rearview mirror. "That true, Crystal? You aren't religious either?"

She thought about it before answering. " I'm just not sure that the Navajo ways have anything to do with me and what I want to be."

"*Where* she wants to be is off the reservation," Holly explained.

"What do you hope to find on the outside?" Ray asked.

"Me," Crystal replied with a smile.

Forty-five minutes later, after picking up Holly's sweater in Farmington, Ray stopped at a self-serve gas station to refuel. While he got out and walked to the pump, Holly turned to look at Crystal. "Do you still want to know where people sell stuff they've stolen?"

"Yeah, why?" Crystal asked.

"I think Ray would help you out if you told him what's going on," Holly said.

Crystal looked over at Junior, who'd been sitting quietly, listening. He shrugged. "This is your call," he said. "But you do need to find the rug fast. If it's resold, you'll never be able to track it down."

Crystal considered it for a moment. "All right. We'll tell Ray. If he knows, or can find out, who deals in stolen property around here, it might lead me to my rug."

When Ray returned to the truck, they were all quiet, waiting for Crystal to speak.

Ray looked around, studying their faces. "Okay, people, what's the deal here? Something going on I should know about?"

Despite her misgivings, Crystal told him what

had happened. "I really need it back. That rug represents months and months of very hard work. Can you help me?"

"Maybe," he said slowly. "I know a guy. . . . But even if it *was* stolen from you and he has it, he won't just turn it over to you. You'll have to buy it back. Or, if we're sure he has it, we could call in the cops."

"Why can't you just talk your friend into returning it to Crystal—providing he has it, of course," Lucinda asked.

"We're *not* friends. I knew a guy who did business with him a while back, and he introduced us," he said. "What I can do for you is make sure he gives you a great price. That may be the easiest and quickest way for you to get your rug back," he added. "But don't get your hopes up too high. Your rug could be anywhere by now."

Crystal wanted to simply be grateful, but she couldn't quite get another very disturbing thought out of her mind. Maybe the reason Ray was so sure the man would give him a good price was because he'd been the one who'd brought the rug to him in the first place. But, for that very reason, she couldn't afford to turn down Ray's help—not if she ever planned on seeing her rug again.

"One more thing," Ray added. "We're going to

need some bills to flash—just so they're sure that we really can afford to buy it back."

Crystal groaned. "I don't even have a dollar with me, just three quarters."

"I've got two dollars," Junior said.

Lucinda stared at her purse. "Look, if you all are willing to forgo the pizza, I can come up with about thirty dollars. You can pay me back later, Crystal, when you sell your rug."

Ray drove directly to a run-down neighborhood near the bridge on the old Bloomfield highway. Judging from the dozens of old cars, all in various stages of disrepair, it was an auto repair shop.

"They stole a rug from me, not our pickup," Crystal said, looking at Ray.

"The building behind this one is supposed to be used for storing car parts, but it's really a pawnshop. Only everything they sell there is hot or at least *very* warm," Ray said and smiled sheepishly.

Holly shot her brother a hard stare. "You know what, Ray? I'm not even going to ask who steered you to this place or why."

"Good," Ray replied, "because I have no intention of telling you. It's all in the past." Ray looked at Crystal. "You ready?"

Junior started to scramble out the tailgate with

her, and Holly and Lucinda began scooting toward the door, but Ray stopped them.

"Whoa! We can't all go in. I'll take Crystal with me, and she and I can handle this. Otherwise it'll look like a school field trip, and we'll never get past the office."

"*I* think we should stick together," Lucinda said. "They won't dare do anything if we have friends with us."

Ray shook his head. "We can't work it that way, trust me. We have to be inconspicuous and get in and out as quickly as possible. They know we're not cops, but if we act like we're going to cause trouble, we'll catch it for sure."

"Are they armed?" Holly whispered.

"They don't need knives or guns. Mikey is the size of a Suburban, and Joe looks like Frankenstein's ugly brother. Either one of those guys could yank off our arms and legs and feed them to us."

Junior's eyes widened slightly. "Then maybe I should go with you. I have a few tricks up my sleeve for getting out of tight spots."

"We can use you, then," Ray said. "You girls stay out here, and lock the door. Mikey's a pig around females. Believe me, you won't like his kind of attention."

Holly shuddered, and Lucinda grimaced. "Okay. We'll stay here."

When Ray put his arm around Crystal's shoulder, Junior stiffened. Noticing Junior's reaction, Ray added, "I'm going to introduce Crystal as my girlfriend and you as her brother."

"But we don't look anything alike," Junior protested.

"To them, all Navajos look the same."

"You didn't tell me they were blind," Junior muttered.

"Trust me, okay?" Ray said. "They're not just stupid, they're dangerous, too."

Junior nodded. "Okay, we'll play along."

Instead of entering through the small garage office, Ray took them inside through an unmarked side door. They were walking down a narrow aisle flanked by shelves of dusty, oily-smelling car parts when the biggest man Crystal had ever seen suddenly came out of a room to their left.

"Hey, Mikey," Ray greeted him.

Seeing Ray, the man broke out into a wide grin. "Hey, Bones."

"Come on, Mikey. I've gained a few pounds," Ray joked.

Crystal looked at Ray, then at Mikey. Ray was

around five foot ten and weighed maybe 170 pounds. Junior and she weren't considered small either, though they didn't weigh anywhere near what Ray did. But in comparison to Mikey they all looked like chihuahuas milling around a Great Dane.

Mikey seemed to be an affable giant, but when he patted Ray on the back, Ray staggered forward a few steps.

"Is this your girl—or his?" Mikey asked.

"Mine. Her name's Chrissy. That's her brother . . . Jay."

"Ray and Jay and Chris-ay. So what brings you here?"

"Chrissy needs some help. Someone lifted the rug she was weaving, and—"

"What's that got to do with me?" Mikey's expression darkened, and Ray automatically took a step back.

Crystal glanced at Junior, and saw him reaching down to his medicine pouch. With her back against the wall and Ray and Junior in front of her, Crystal had nowhere to run. "If you know who might be willing to deal, I thought I could try to buy it back," Crystal said.

"Oh, you think maybe I could serve as your broker? That I might be able to do," Mikey said, relaxing.

As he led the way farther into the building, an

Anglo man with dirty-looking dark hair appeared, and the word *troll* immediately leapt into Crystal's mind. His shirt was halfway open, revealing what looked a lot like a gorilla's chest, and his powerful arms were almost black with hair.

"What's this?" he asked. "Are we baby-sitters now?" His voice was deep—like the sound of distant thunder.

Mikey explained, but instead of relaxing, Joe's eyes flashed with fire. "We buy and sell merchandise here, Ray, and we don't get involved with anyone else's problems."

"I know. I don't expect you to give us something for nothing. We brought money. But I'm hoping that, if you have what she's looking for, you'll give her a good price," Ray said.

"What is it you're looking for?" Joe asked, his beady black eyes suddenly trained on Crystal.

She felt like a rabbit in front of a snake. "A large wool rug in a Chief's Blanket pattern."

"That means nothing to me. What color?"

"Red, blue, black, and white."

Joe mulled it over, scratching his neck, which needed a shave. "I have a Navajo rug here, and it's got red in it, but I'm not sure about the other colors. Since it's damaged I can give you a great deal."

"Damaged?" Crystal's voice wavered slightly.

"That's right. There's a stain in the middle—like wine or grape juice."

Crystal was sure she was going to be sick. *Grape juice?* If that was her rug, she *would* get sick.

"Can she take a look at it?" Ray asked.

Joe nodded to Mikey, who turned and walked down the hall in the direction Joe had come from.

Crystal tried not to scream while Ray and Joe made small talk about some major-league baseball team. It was taking forever for Mikey to return, and patience had never been one of her strong points.

Mikey finally came back, a big-rolled up rug slung over his massive shoulder.

"I took a quick look at it back there. It's got this huge splotch in the middle, but I don't think it's grape juice. It may be dog pee and that made the colors run. It smells really funky."

Mikey tossed the rug on the floor and unrolled it with a good kick.

Crystal closed her eyes, then with a burst of courage opened them again. It wasn't her rug. All of a sudden she could breathe again. But the minute she took a deep breath, she regretted it. The most wretched scent emanated from the rug.

"That's no dog, that's a skunk," she managed, then nearly gagged.

"Yeah, you're probably right. We left it outside

last night, and I think we had a little visitor." Joe pulled up his shirt and tried to breathe through the fabric. "So, do you want it? You can take it off our hands for just fifty bucks."

She held her breath, and shook her head, trying to figure out what was more disgusting—the putrid rug or Joe's hairy, fat belly, now showing because he'd pulled up his shirt.

Ray had one hand over his mouth. "Thanks for your help anyway," he said, backing up, then rushing back in the direction they'd come. Junior grabbed Crystal's hand and pulled her along with him.

Mikey followed. "Why don't you check out Jerry Albert over at Hudson's Trading Post. I heard he's selling a rug that's so hot it's on fire. Apparently the owner is checking out every business in the Four Corners trying to track it down."

Crystal looked at Ray. "Get me back to the rez."

Chapter Eleven

RAY SHRUGGED at Mikey, then they all strode quickly back to the truck. Once they were inside and on the road again, he slumped back against the seat. "Phew! That was some scent. I don't see how skunks can stand each other."

"I agree. But thankfully it wasn't my rug that got sprayed!" Crystal said, then explained to Holly and Lucinda what had happened.

"Mr. Albert, *a thief?*" Lucinda said, and shook her head. "I just don't believe it. Maybe that moose of a guy has him confused with somebody else."

"I hope so," Holly said. "Mr. Albert's never even overcharged anyone, not as far as I know anyway, and he's really nice."

"Sorry, guys, but Mikey's information is usually right on the money," Ray said.

"Then drop me off by the trading post, Ray. I want to check things out," Crystal said.

Junior looked at her, and even though he hadn't

said a word, she knew exactly what was bothering him. They'd searched the place once before and not found anything.

"Do you two need our help once we get there?" Ray asked.

"No. In fact it'll be better if it's just Junior and me. Mr. Albert is used to seeing us there," Crystal explained.

As they drew closer to the trading post, traffic changed drastically. Tribal police cars, sirens wailing, whipped past them at high speed.

"What the heck's going on?" Holly asked, stretching her neck to look down the highway.

"A traffic accident, maybe?" Lucinda shrugged. "I hope not."

Ten minutes later, as they approached the turnoff from the main highway, they could see flashing lights a half mile down the gravel road.

"Whatever's going on, it's happening at Hudson's Trading Post," Ray said, then slowing down, pulled over to the shoulder of the road. "Look, guys, I've been trying to avoid the cops ever since I got into trouble. I'll be happy to drop you off at your doorstep, Crystal, but this is as close as I'm getting to Hudson's."

"That's fine. We can walk from here," Junior said.

"Sure. And thanks for everything," Crystal said, opening the tailgate and scrambling down out of the truck.

"Let us know what happens," Holly called out.

"Wait," Ray said. "I'll tell you what. We'll meet you at the highway next to the big sign in say, twenty minutes? That way if you find you need a ride someplace else, you'll have a way to get there."

"That would be great. Thanks," Crystal said. As soon as Junior and she closed the tailgate, Ray wasted no time putting some distance between himself and the tribal police.

Crystal and Junior walked quickly down the dusty road to Hudson's. "There are four tribal police cars right outside the entrance," she noted as they reached the parking lot. "What do you think is going on?"

"I'm not sure. But I've got to tell you, Birdie, I'd really hate to find out that someone died in there," he whispered.

"You don't believe in that stuff about the *chindi*, do you?" Crystal asked, then smacked herself on the head. "Sorry! Of course you do."

"Hey, even Anglos believe in good and bad spirits. The difference between us is that our versions of heaven and hell are different. We believe that the good side of a person merges with universal harmony, but the bad side becomes a *chindi* and stays earth-bound, waiting to make problems for the living." Junior stopped a good fifty yards from the trading post. "Until I'm sure that there hasn't been a death there and the place isn't contaminated by the *chindi*, this is as far as I go. You'll do the same if you have any sense."

"You've known me all my life. When have you ever believed I had any sense?" Crystal asked with a smile. "Wait here and I'll be back in a few minutes."

Before he could stop her, she hurried to the trading post. As she stepped quietly onto the porch, Crystal discovered two tribal police officers in their khaki uniforms standing just outside the entrance, having a conversation. Stopping by one of the porch supports, partially blocked from their view, she stood motionless and listened.

"I'm glad we were able to make this arrest. It's really getting sad when wannabees are ripping off our own healers to get ranked into Shiprock gangs. At least this kid tried to sell it at Hudson's instead of that place in Waterflow—what's the guy's name, Sanders?"

"What wrong with Sanders?" the other officer asked.

"Nothing, officially. We haven't been able to prove he's a fence. Now he's started peddling Navajo merchandise over the Internet. That's just going to make our job a lot harder. Tracking down stolen property that has already been shipped across the country is going to be a rough deal."

"What are we doing to get enough evidence to make an arrest?"

"The usual—dropping by at random times, looking over his merchandise and comparing it with our hot sheets, like that. But so far we haven't had any hits," the officer answered.

The officers stopped talking when another officer came outside, manhandling a Navajo boy about seventeen who was trying to squirm loose despite being in handcuffs.

The two outside officers stepped over and grabbed the boy by each arm, lifting him off the ground slightly. Their shaven-headed prisoner, wearing very baggy pants, a web belt, and a black T-shirt, cursed and stopped squirming.

As Crystal stepped back off the porch, the officer who'd just come outside noticed her and caught her eye.

He motioned for the others to continue, then came over to where she was standing. "What's your name and your business here, young lady?"

"Crystal Manyfeathers," she answered. "I . . . uh . . . wanted to talk to Mr. Albert, the trader."

"Do you know the boy with the officers, Crystal?" He turned and motioned toward the squad car, where the officers were busy placing their prisoner into the backseat.

"No. He's not from around here, sir," Crystal answered.

The officer watched her for a moment, and she tried not to look nervous. Finally he spoke. "Mr. Albert's busy at the moment. What did you need to see him about?"

"I'm a weaver. He's going to be selling one of my rugs," she said, but didn't explain further.

The officer nodded. "Maybe you should come back another time, Miss Manyfeathers."

"Let her through, officer."

Crystal recognized Mr. Albert's voice. As she looked past a fourth officer in the doorway, who was as wide as a tree trunk and just about as gnarly looking, she saw Mr. Albert standing inside.

The officer, holding a small tan, black, and white rug draped over his arm, came out and held the screen door open for Crystal. "Thanks," she said, then joined Mr. Albert. "What's going on?"

"I was approached by the boy you saw being taken into custody. He came in and said he had a rug to sell, but was so nervous I knew something wasn't right. There was another customer in the store at the time, so I used her as an excuse and told the kid to come back in an hour. After he left, I called the police. The officers waited in the back, then came out after he returned with the goods and made his pitch. The rug had already been reported stolen, so the police knew what to look for."

"Was it the one the officer had?" Crystal asked, disappointed that it obviously wasn't hers.

"Yes. The officers have to lock it up for now as evidence."

"Sometimes doing the right thing can be expensive. I mean, I'm sure you could have made good money selling a collector something that had belonged to a medicine man," Crystal said, wondering if that was the only thing Mr. Albert had received that was stolen.

"Maybe. But had I done business with a thief, I wouldn't have liked myself very much. And that would have been hard, considering I've got to look at myself in the mirror every single morning." He added with a smile, "Life's a lot simpler when you deal fairly and honestly with people."

"The thief didn't know you, did he?" Crystal asked, trying to figure out how Mikey had gotten the wrong impression of Mr. Albert.

"No. The way he talked I think he brought that rug to me by mistake. Someone in Farmington who didn't deal in high-priced merchandise sent him here. But either the kid or the fence got me mixed up with the two merchants in this area who are known for not asking questions about any Navajo-made items."

"Who are they?"

He shook his head. "It's not for me to name names. But one of these days they'll get caught. It's as inevitable as sunset."

"I'm glad you're the one who's getting my rug, Mr. Albert."

He nodded. "So am I. But remember I'll need it soon."

With a nod, Crystal turned and left the store. The officers had driven away, but Junior was waiting down the road. His hand was resting on his medicine pouch as she approached. "They just brought out that boy. What did he do?" he called out to her before she could get near.

"Nobody died, you can relax. Mr. Albert called the police on that kid. He came down from Shiprock and tried to sell a rug he stole from a *hataalii.* Is your dad missing anything? I heard that to get ranked into a gang some of the boys have to steal something from one of our medicine men."

Junior shook his head. "No one's stolen anything from us, unless it happened while I was gone today.

But there are lots of other medicine men on the rez, and I know that at least two live around Shiprock," he said. After a pause, he added, "Does this mean you've ruled out Mr. Albert?"

"Definitely, but while I was there, I did find out a couple of interesting things. First, there's a shop owner the cops are checking up on in Waterflow, probably the same place Mikey had in mind. The owner's name is Sanders. One of the officers said that Sanders deals a lot through the Internet. Also, I found out from Mr. Albert that there's another merchant in this area who doesn't really care where his suppliers get their stuff. Mr. Albert didn't want to tell me who it was, but I'm betting it's Mr. Wilkinson. I don't know of any other merchant between Shiprock and Gallup who deals with Indian crafts, do you?"

He shook his head. "I'm almost afraid to ask, but what do you want to do next?"

"Ask Ray for a ride again."

"I know he's helped us today, but Ray's trouble waiting to happen, Birdie. Are you sure you want to get him involved?"

"Unless you can think of another way to get us to Waterflow, we don't have a choice," she answered. "And do I have to remind you that time's passing and I've got to have that rug by the time I go to bed tonight? It's not even finished yet, and my ceremony starts Saturday!"

"All right," he said.

"Good, that's settled. Now let's get going."

Ray, Holly, and Lucinda pulled up beside the turnoff just as Junior and Crystal reached the highway. The five were on the way to Waterflow several minutes later. Crystal had told the others what she'd heard the officers saying, and Ray had immediately confirmed the police's suspicions about Sanders.

"I heard that Mike Sanders fences stuff, though not on Mikey's level. But he's worth checking out. I've never met the guy, but maybe with my street smarts and your brains, we can make it work. What do you say, Crystal?"

Ray winked at her, and Crystal smiled back. "Let's give it a try," she said.

"Why not save time by going in and telling him straight out what you're looking for?" Junior asked.

"We're not tracking down which kid ended up with your basketball, Junior. This is the real world now, and you've got to start thinking like an adult," Ray said.

Crystal noticed how Ray had just talked down to Junior, despite the fact that there was less than three years' difference between them.

She glanced at Junior to see how he was taking it, and saw a neutral expression on his face. That wasn't good. When Junior hid what he was thinking, it usually meant that there was a lot going on in his head.

Waterflow was an old farming community located mostly along the north side of the San Juan River. Many of the apple orchards and alfalfa fields remained, but in the last few years, dozens had been subdivided into small lots for fancy homes. Crystal hated to see the change, having enjoyed the pheasants and ducks in the fields a lot more than the boxlike homes that seemed to pop up out of nowhere, like mushrooms in tall, damp grass.

When they reached Sanders Southwest Treasures, a small, solid-looking cinder block shop with a green roof and iron grilles across the windows, Ray parked in the three-car parking lot, then turned around to Crystal. "Hey, girl, do you want to pose as my girlfriend again? I think we're getting pretty good at it."

"Sure." Crystal didn't have to look at Junior's expression to know that Ray's latest comment would only make things worse.

"Let's go give this a try," Ray said, opening his door.

“I’m going with you,” Junior said, heading for the tailgate.

“Bad idea, Junior. I have no idea what’s inside. You’d be better off staying here and being our back-up,” Ray said.

Junior shook his head. “I’m going.”

As Crystal and Junior climbed out of the back, Holly and Lucinda got out as well. “We’re going to take a look around,” Holly whispered, pointing toward a shed in the back. “Maybe he keeps some of his merchandise in there—the kind he doesn’t want anyone to see. It’s probably locked, but maybe we can see through the windows.”

“Be careful nosing around, okay? Sanders doesn’t have the same reputation as Mikey, but if he’s dealing with stolen stuff he’s not exactly harmless either,” Ray whispered back.

Once they’d split up, Ray placed his arm around Crystal’s shoulders. “We have to make it look good.”

Junior glared at him but didn’t say a word, and that worried Crystal even more. But with more pressing things on her mind, she concentrated on the job at hand.

They went inside the dimly lit shop. Across the length of the room were three large glass display cases that served as both a long counter and a barrier between the customer area and an open work area with packing boxes and mailing supplies. A section of the counter lifted up to allow someone to pass through. The cases held everything from turquoise jewelry to pottery and small wooden and metal sculptures. On the walls were a few Navajo rugs, paintings of the Southwest, and shelves of carved and cast figures of horses, cowboys, and Plains Indians in warbonnets. In one corner was a small room with a half-open door that appeared to be a closet, and beside it was a large table stacked with boxes apparently ready to be shipped.

They had just stepped to the counter to see if anything was behind it and out of view when a tall, slender Anglo man with dark hair in a ponytail came out of the office. "What can I do for you three?" he asked briskly.

Crystal saw him studying her and felt creeped out all of a sudden. She looked away, verifying again that her rug wasn't hung on the wall someplace.

"We're looking for a rug," Ray answered.

The man's gaze stayed on Crystal. "Hey, you aren't Crystal Manyfeathers, are you?"

She looked up at him in surprise. "Yes. We haven't met before, have we?"

He shook his head. "I do a little business with

Jerry Albert from time to time and he pointed you out. I've seen some of your small practice rugs. I would be happy to carry your work here if you'd like to do business with me sometime."

Crystal looked around the store. "But you don't seem to carry many rugs," she said.

"Most of what I sell is through mail order, so I don't worry about keeping a large inventory on display here. My clients tell me what they want and then I track it down for them or custom order it from a craftsman. If you worked with me, you'd be asked to use certain color schemes at times, or maybe work up a specific design. You'd be well paid, of course, but you'd have to be real professional about it, keeping deadlines and maintaining quality."

"Could you give me an example of the type of rugs you normally sell?" Crystal asked.

"Sure. Let me bring out the one I was about to pack up. Wait here."

As he went into the back Ray looked at her and smiled. "Smooth, Crystal."

She felt her cheeks grow hot. "Thanks."

Sanders joined them a moment later carrying a small rolled-up rug. "My clients from California like Navajo rugs that use warm colors, like this Ganado red."

Crystal looked at the rug, then back at him. The fringes on the end and the loose weave made it clear to her that the rug had been made in Mexico, not by any Navajo weaver.

"Are you selling this one as a Navajo rug?"

"Kind of pretty, isn't it?" he asked, hedging her question.

She didn't answer. "Where do you normally get your rugs? Ganado? Tuba City? Chinle?"

"Here and there. I go all over the rez, and if I can't find what I want I go to other wholesalers. I've bought from both Jerry Albert and Roger Wilkinson on occasion."

"Wilkinson sells rugs?" Ray asked. "I've been in his trading post once or twice, but I don't remember seeing any."

"From what I hear he keeps a tight inventory, only buying up rugs and pottery that he's sure he can move out fast, so he may not have much on hand. All I know for sure is that he favors rugs like this one with bold colors, and small pots with low prices because he caters mostly to the tourist trade. I bought a rug from him only yesterday—it's exactly what one of my customers had asked for, and priced right. It's not the quality I normally expect, but it'll serve the client, I'm sure."

"Is it another Ganado red?" Crystal asked.

"No, this particular client wanted something with some blue in the weave and wasn't too concerned with the pattern."

"May I see it?" Crystal asked. Her own rug had incorporated blue tones and it was worth a look, just in case.

"Sure." He brought out the rug, but it was much smaller than hers and woven with lots of chevrons and diamonds. Although there was no doubt that it was a Navajo rug, it had been hastily woven. Crystal was sure that if she tried she'd be able to stick her finger completely through the weaving—something you could never do with a rug from a good weaver.

"Wilkinson called last night, and I understand he's got another one almost ready to sell that's a real masterpiece. I've already told him I'm interested in taking a look. I don't normally buy rugs unless I've received an order, but if it's half as good as Wilkinson says, I'll make an exception. I'm just waiting for it to be finished."

Crystal glanced at Junior and then forced herself to smile calmly at Sanders. "Thanks so much for taking time to talk to us."

As they walked outside, Ray pushed Junior aside, then put his arm around Crystal and gave her a squeeze. "You did great!"

"Thanks," she said. As she looked for Junior, she realized that he'd moved around behind them and was now on her other side. For the first time today he took her hand, then helped her up into the back of the pickup. "I know you're thinking Wilkinson has your rug, Birdie," Junior said, "but just remember that we don't know that for sure. There are several excellent weavers on the rez."

"I know, but we have to check it out." She looked at Ray, hoping he'd volunteer to drive them there, since it was almost five now. But Ray had started sneezing. His eyes had turned red and were watering heavily.

"I think I'm allergic to something inside the store," Ray grumbled, then went into another sneezing fit that lasted for about half a minute.

Lucinda and Holly were already back in the truck, and as soon as they were all ready to go, Holly gave them an update. "We struck out. There was nothing in that shed except an old display case and some rusted-out metal shelving."

Crystal told them what had happened, as Ray continued blowing his nose and grumbling about allergies. She had to talk loudly to be heard over the noise he was making. When he finally stopped sneezing, Crystal glanced over at him. "Can you give us a ride to Mr. Wilkinson's?"

"Yeah, but I've got to go home first. My nose is running like crazy, and I'm getting a headache. I need an allergy pill and an aspirin."

"Can you drop me off first? I have an appointment in Shiprock," Holly said, then checked her watch. "And could you hurry? I'm going to be late."

"Your job—I forgot!" Ray said, checking his own watch. "Don't worry. We'll go there right now."

"You got a job?" Crystal asked.

Holly shot her brother a dirty look. "Thanks a lot, Ray," she muttered.

Ray sneezed again, then blew his nose. "Sorry, Red."

"Tell us about your job, Holly," Lucinda said. "Come on."

"I had to pay for my sweater somehow," Holly said. "Then I found out that one of the ladies from our church needed a housekeeper. Unfortunately I couldn't just clean her house once and then quit. So I agreed to take the job and work one day a week after school until her daughter comes home from college for the summer."

"That doesn't sound so bad!" Crystal said, relieved to finally have learned where the money for Holly's sweater had come from. "But why did you keep it from everyone?"

"My parents don't know about it yet and I didn't

want them to find out until I earned enough to get the sweater. They wanted me to focus on school because my grades are slipping."

"Your secret is safe with us, Holly," Crystal said, looking around at the others and seeing them nod. "But you'd better let them know before they find out from somebody else."

Fifteen minutes later, after dropping Holly off at her workplace in Shiprock, and Lucinda at her home close to the highway, Ray pulled up beside the road.

"Hey, guys, do you mind if I drop you off here?" Ray wheezed, his voice raw and his nose red. "I need to take something for this sneezing before I die."

"Just open the window and relax, Ray. You'll feel better by the time you get home," Junior said.

"Easy for you to say," Ray grumbled. "My nose is about to explode."

Crystal glanced over at Junior, suspecting he'd had something to do with Ray's sudden attack of allergies outside Mike Sanders's business, but Junior's face was a portrait of innocence.

Chapter Twelve

FIVE MINUTES later, Junior and Crystal were walking alone on the narrow gravel road that would eventually take them to Wilkinson's Trading Post. That solitary shop was farther south, about two miles from the highway in a low, arid valley. A spring there, surrounded by cottonwoods, provided water for Navajos for miles around. To their west, the foothills of the nearby mountains rose high above the desert floor, and piñon and juniper trees dotted the landscape in far greater numbers. Cloud shadows created a few dark splotches on the hills, but it didn't really look like rain today.

"Do you like Ray?" Junior was the first to break the silence between them, though they'd already been walking for five minutes.

"He's nice, and I appreciate what he did today, driving us around and all that."

"That's not what I meant," Junior said in a low voice.

"I know. But I do believe I answered your question," she said. Out of the corner of her eye she saw Junior smile.

They walked quietly for several more minutes, climbing the long hill that preceded the downward slope into the valley beyond. Finally Crystal spoke again. "What am I going to do if we strike out at Mr. Wilkinson's? I love weaving. It's almost as if it's a part of me."

"It is . . . or was," he answered.

Crystal gave him a look filled with curiosity, but before she could ask him about his comment, he continued.

"If we don't find the rug," he said, "we'll have to come up with another way for you to stop falling asleep when you weave."

"Is there one?"

"Not that I know of right now, but we'll figure something out."

"I really appreciate you standing by me through all this, Junior. You've been terrific."

"You and I are friends . . . special friends. I may not agree with the way you think, but I . . . like you."

Crystal smiled. "I like you, too," she answered.

He smiled again, but they avoided looking directly at each other until, at long last, Wilkinson's

Trading Post came into view at the foot of the hill. She was gazing at the low, flat-roofed building, smaller than Hudson's but with an equally large covered porch in front of the entrance, when Junior suddenly stopped walking and pointed to the ground.

"Look over there by the side of the road," he said. "On the shoulder."

Crystal could see the tracks of a vehicle that obviously had been pulling a trailer. The driver had pulled off the road for some reason before continuing on his journey. "Wilkinson has a trailer," she told him. "Lucinda already told me about that. And it looks like he used it recently. Will you help me distract him so I can look around?"

"If I can," Junior said, then looked up and listened. "Someone's coming on horseback."

She looked down the road both ways. "Where?"

He motioned behind them with a tilt of his head. A heartbeat later she heard the sound of a horse loping over the hill, but off the road, on the softer shoulder among the tufts of grama grass.

"How do you *do* that?" she asked, turning around to see who it was.

"Oh-oh," he muttered a breath later as the rider appeared, silhouetted against the sky. "It's Biggins, and he sees us."

Her eyes grew wide. "Do you think he'll try to pound us both into the ground right here and now?"

"He might *try*," he said, his hand dropping to his medicine pouch. "But it's time for the battle between us to stop. If we intend to survive this school year, we need to turn him into a friend instead of an enemy."

"Yeah, but how are we going to do that?"

"I have an idea, but there's not enough time to explain. No matter what happens, let kindness guide your actions. Then the problem will resolve itself."

"What? Kind, how?" she asked. Biggins had slowed his horse to a walk now, angling toward them as they stood beside the road.

"Remember our origin stories. Talking God and Calling God were furious at Dawn Boy once, but it was Dawn Boy's kindness that saved the day."

Crystal recalled the story only vaguely. All she knew for sure was that it was sung during the Night Chant and dealt with Dawn Boy's wanderings. Making a mental note to ask him about it later, and hoping that she'd be able to figure out what to do next, Crystal stood beside Junior. Biggins dismounted with a dusty thud, dropping the reins.

She hoped her shaking hands weren't obvious as she smiled and waved. "Hi."

"I'm glad I ran into you," Biggins said, glaring at Crystal beneath the brim of his sweat-stained Stetson. "I found out that it was *your* mess on the floor that caused my accident."

"Yeah—*accident*," Crystal said, standing up straight, her hands on her hips. "Obviously I didn't do it on purpose, and if you remember right, I warned you to stop." Biggins took a step toward her. "Get over it," she added. "Accidents happen."

As Biggins moved closer, Junior tried to step between them, but Crystal sidestepped in the opposite direction, keeping clear. There was no way she'd allow Junior to get into a fight with Biggins because of her.

As she stood her ground she heard—or thought she heard—Junior muttering a Good Luck Song under his breath.

Suddenly Biggins's expression changed from anger to annoyance, and she saw him desperately trying to force his fingers beneath the cast on his wrist.

"Why does it always have to itch *beneath* this stupid cast? I hate that!"

Distracted, Biggins began tapping and rapping against the cast, trying to reach between his wrist and the cast with his big, stubby fingers, but failing. "This is all your fault, Crystal."

Crystal looked over at Junior, remembering Ray's sneezing fit. Her friend looked concerned, sympathetic, and completely innocent.

Recalling what Junior had told her about showing kindness, Crystal looked around on the ground and found a long thin twig. She picked it up, brushed off the sand, and held it out to Biggins. "I think this'll reach down inside and relieve that itch," she said.

He grabbed the slender stick and slipped it under the cast. A second later, he smiled with relief. "Ahh. Thanks!"

Junior plucked some dry leaves off a small plant growing by the roadside and crumbled them into the palm of his hand. "Let me see your arm. I have something that might help with the irritation."

Biggins stopped scratching with the branch and held out his arm tentatively.

Junior said a brief prayer, then slipped some of the leaf fragments beneath the cast. "Work it down toward the itchy spot with the end of the stick. The leaves are called *Azee'ntl'iní*, gummy medicine. It's used as a dusting powder sometimes. It'll soothe your skin, like baby powder. No offense."

"I think it's helping," Biggins said, working the leaf fragments around carefully.

"Good," Junior said. "I thought it might. My dad may be able to give you something more powerful if you go talk to him, but that'll hold you for now."

Biggins stared at his cast for several moments, then looked at Junior. "Thanks for helping me out, bud. What can I do for you in return?"

Junior looked at Crystal and, when she nodded, told Biggins about Crystal's stolen rug and how she had been trying to check out suspects, especially anyone who owned a horse trailer. "We're on our way to Wilkinson's Trading Post. Is there anything we should know about him that might help us?"

Biggins's expression darkened and he adjusted his hat while he thought about it. "Be very careful when you deal with him. He can come across as a very bad dude when he gets riled. I've even heard that some of his older customers are afraid of him." He paused, then looked at Crystal. "Do you think he's the one who stole your rug?"

"I don't know, but that's why we're going over there to look around. I don't think he knows what I look like, so that should make it easier," she said.

Biggins looked back at Junior. "If you have a problem with him, just come over to my house. We'll go together then and I'll back you up," he said. "Oh, and keep this in mind. He's paranoid about teenagers hanging around in his store. He'll probably watch you both like a hawk."

"Thanks for the heads up," Crystal said. Biggins wasn't so bad after all. Up to now, she'd never suspected him of being anything more than a bulldozer in cleats. His human side had come as a surprise to her. Somewhere beneath all that bulk pounded a good heart.

As Biggins rode off, Junior smiled at her. "You did a great job of turning his anger around."

"Junior, I'm confused. How could you have possibly known that he'd have an itch beneath his cast and we'd be able to help him?"

"Remember when Shorty broke his leg last year? He had the same problem whenever he worked up a sweat."

She narrowed her eyes. "So you counted on the same thing happening now? That's stretching coincidence. And what about Ray's sudden sneezing attack, and how is it that you *always* hear things before anyone else does?"

He gave her a slow smile. "A smart Navajo never reveals his secrets."

Crystal sighed softly. She should have known she wouldn't get a straight answer. "Tell me more about Dawn Boy. I couldn't remember the whole story. I had to wing it once Biggins showed up."

He chuckled softly. "Good thing you're an expert at that." Seeing her scowl, he grew serious and began. "One day during his wanderings, Dawn Boy found himself at Canyon de Chelly."

Power and magic laced through Junior's words, making the wonder of days gone by seem as real as the desert around them. "There, he spotted a hogan with black prayer sticks at each side of the blanket-covered door. Sprinkling pollen before him to light his way, he went through the doorway without waiting for an invitation. Soon Talking God and Calling God became aware of him and were outraged that he'd come into their presence without permission.

"Dawn Boy faced their anger bravely and told them that he'd come with gifts. After giving them his offerings, he sang a song. Dawn Boy's ability to keep his head and his reliance on the Navajo Songs was rewarded, and instead of making enemies, Dawn Boy turned them into his friends. When he left them to continue his journey, he walked with beauty around him."

"You've learned a lot, Junior," Crystal said, clearly impressed.

"The hardest thing was finding my own way of telling stories so I wasn't just paraphrasing my dad. Stories are supposed to change a little each time they're told. Every storyteller can bring a new insight or outlook to it because the stories are alive—all knowledge is. But I still have a long way to go before I'm as good as my dad. And sometimes I get impatient just like you because it takes so much time to learn it all."

"Yeah, but unlike me, you always keep it under control and do the right thing anyway."

His eyebrows went up. "So you're ready to admit you were wrong not to put in a spirit line?"

She hesitated before answering him. "I regret doing it because of all the trouble it caused," she replied honestly. "I guess it's like the school counselor always says, actions have consequences—and my action had a lot more consequences than I ever dreamed."

Entering the parking area in front of Wilkinson's Trading Post, she suddenly stopped in midstride as someone came out the entrance. "Hey, isn't that Shorty?"

Junior saw his friend and waved. Shorty looked at them, did a surprised double-take, then jogged over, smiling. "Hey, what are you two doing down here?"

Crystal told him about her missing rug. It obviously didn't matter much now who knew. She'd followed every clue she could come up with. If she didn't find it either today or tomorrow, then she'd have to accept that it was long gone, probably out of her reach, and she'd never see it again.

"Let me help you guys out with this," Shorty said quickly. "Coyote—that's what some of us call Wilkinson—is a cheat. I came 'cause my dad had pawned his turquoise and silver watch here, and now that he finally got paid, Dad sent me over here to get it out of hock. But Mr. Wilkinson wants three times what he paid my dad for it. He double-talked me with some legal bull I couldn't understand, so I couldn't argue back. Dad's never going to be able to get it back at that price, and that's the watch Granddad made for him."

"I'm sorry, Shorty," Crystal said. "I sure wish your father had gone to Mr. Albert. At least he's fair. My dad borrowed money from him one time so we could buy some ewes for breeding stock, and he used my mom's squash-blossom necklace as security. But he got it back without any problem." She sighed softly. "Lots of families around here borrow money by pawning things. It's easier than trying to get a bank to help," Crystal said. "But why did your dad go to Mr. Wilkinson—Coyote—if he has such a bad reputation?"

"Dad knew that Coyote has a Web site, and he was hoping he'd be able to do some business with him, making jewelry to sell through the Internet. You know my dad's a silversmith." Shorty glanced back at the trading post with disdain and added, "Anyway, if you think he has your rug, I'm ready to help."

"While Birdie looks around for her rug, I'm going to try and keep him distracted," Junior said. "But just in case Wilkinson catches on to us, we need someone out here who can go for help."

"I'm your man. I'll hang outside, and if you're not out in twenty minutes, I'll go get help."

"That's great, Shorty," Crystal said. "We talked to Biggins a while ago, and he said he'd come over if we needed backup. You know where he lives, right?"

"Everyone knows where Biggins lives. But are you sure about that? I thought he wanted to stuff you both into a trash can."

Junior smiled. "We settled that. Just get somebody here who can bail us out if we need it."

"Take care, you two." Shorty nodded, then walked over and sat down on the edge of the porch.

Junior and Crystal walked inside the trading post, which smelled of fresh paint. It was well lit and much brighter than Mr. Albert's place. There were large circular mirrors up high against the ceiling in every corner, reminding her of a big convenience store. To their left were metal shelves filled with stacks of jeans, shirts, and other folded clothes, and to the right, a grocery section with canned and boxed foods.

The clerk, a young Anglo man, came out from behind the counter. "Can I help you find something?"

Crystal looked at him and smiled brightly. "We just wanted to look around. My family's moving a few miles south of this trading post, so we'll probably be shopping here instead of at Hudson's. Mom wanted me to see what you had that Hudson's didn't. I'm also supposed to check out your prices. Do you mind?"

"No, not at all. Go ahead and look around all you want," he said, and smiled pleasantly.

"Are you Mr. Wilkinson?" Crystal asked. She knew he wasn't but she wanted to get the clerk talking. She'd sensed his interest in her and was hoping that Junior would catch on and go look around while she kept him busy.

"Yeah—well, one of them. I'm Bobby Wilkinson. My dad owns the trading post," he said. "What's your name?"

"Crystal Manyfeathers." She gave Junior a quick glance and saw the scowl on his face. She suddenly realized that he wasn't viewing the clerk's interest in her as an opportunity—he was actually jealous! She started to smile, then caught herself and focused her attention on Bobby. "This is a much cleaner-looking trading post than Hudson's. It looks like you stock a lot more merchandise, too."

"I know we do," Bobby agreed with a smile. "Where do you go to school, Crystal?"

Before she could answer, she saw Junior raise one hand to his mouth, as if he were about to cough, then suddenly they heard an ear-shattering squeal from the back of the store.

"It sounds like one of those feral cats has sneaked into the store again." Bobby looked toward the rear of the building, then glanced back to her. "Excuse me a moment, Crystal. I'm going to try and run it out of here before Dad gets back."

As Bobby grabbed a broom and ran off down the main aisle, Crystal looked at Junior, who at the moment looked inordinately pleased with himself. "Nice work. I've got to learn how to do that."

He nodded. "Start looking around. I'll keep him going from place to place while you search."

"Right," she answered.

Crystal walked down a long aisle perpendicular to the one that Wilkinson's son had taken, moving past the dry goods and hardware. In the center of the far wall was a narrow hallway with a sign that said EMPLOYEES ONLY.

Ignoring the sign, Crystal tiptoed past a closed door with a red-lettered sign that said OFFICE. That was too risky to enter, but farther down were three closed doors—one big and heavy, made of metal, which was obviously a walk-in cooler.

Crystal stopped by the first room and tried the door handle. Inside was a wide table stacked with twenty or so hand-woven rugs that were about six feet long or smaller. Checking quickly though the pile, she noticed they were all "commercial grade," meaning that the design had no particular significance, and more attention had been given to the colors than anything else. She remembered hearing that Wilkinson sold mostly to tourists. At the back of the room was a small desk that held a laptop computer and a phone.

As Crystal stepped back out into the hall, watching in both directions for any sign of the clerk, she heard a jarring screech and knew Junior was still keeping Bobby busy. The second room appeared to be a storeroom. There were no windows here, so she had to turn on the light. She searched the area quickly but found nothing except pallets of canned food and soft drinks, mostly colas.

Crystal swallowed back tears of frustration. She took a deep breath, then got ready to join Junior at the front of the store. He'd probably used all the calls he knew by now. As she slipped out of the storeroom, she saw the final door—the one leading to the walk-in cooler.

Deciding she should check in there, too, she stepped down the hall and peered through the thick glass window of the cooler. On the floor against a metal rack containing cartons of eggs, cheese, and cartons of produce, was something rolled up in a blue plastic tarp. Crates of apples were stacked beside it.

She stared at the long tubular package. No food she knew was *that* size and shape—except maybe a humongous sausage. Her heart began drumming frantically as she allowed herself to hope just once more.

Crystal reached for the long handle and pulled the heavy door open with a loud click. As she stepped in, she felt a sudden chill, and it wasn't just from the forty-degree temperature inside. Crystal had suddenly realized that Junior had stopped making his array of odd sounds. Either he'd been forced to try another diversion, or something had gone terribly wrong. But she couldn't stop now. This would only take a minute, and she had to know what was inside the tarp.

Crystal pulled the door closed as much as she could without clicking the latch, then ducked down to check the object out. The plastic seemed to be embedded with tough fibers, much like strapping tape, and wouldn't tear at all.

She brought a ballpoint pen out of her pocket and poked a hole in the material, working the fibers aside to enlarge the opening. A heartbeat later Crystal gasped. It was a rug!

The colors of the wool looked right, but she still couldn't tell if it was hers or not. Hands shaking and her heart beating overtime, Crystal worked clumsily with the pen, trying to rip enough of the plastic away to make sure. Finding the end of the rug, she slit the tarp lengthwise, working between the tough fibers, and checked the weave. The edging cord looked right, and the binding twine that had held the rug to the dowel was still in place. She wouldn't have to unroll it now to check. It was *her* rug!

"Yes!" she said out loud. Then, before she could take her next breath, she heard a hard click. As she turned her head, she saw that someone had shut the door to the cooler.

"No!" Crystal leaped up and pulled the handle,

but it wouldn't budge. She pushed the knob on the metal door below a decal that said EMERGENCY, but nothing happened. Crystal looked through the glass in the door, but all she could see was an empty hallway and a closed door at the store end of the passage.

Crystal turned completely around, looking at the metal walls behind the shelves of food. It was a sealed compartment except for a small vent in the wall up at the top. There was no way to force the door, and even if she could break the glass somehow, the opening was too small to crawl through. She was trapped.

Chapter Thirteen

CRYSTAL CALLED for help, yelling at the top of her lungs, but no one came. Turning back to look down at her rug, Crystal began to cry. She'd found it, but now there was a very real chance that she'd never get her rug, or herself, out of here. Maybe Wilkinson had decided to keep her locked up, take out the rug and destroy it, then let her go. After that, it would all come down to her word against his. Or maybe he was planning on getting rid of her, knowing he'd be exposed as a thief and could end up in jail. Crystal wasn't just afraid anymore, she was terrified.

Shaking badly, she took a while to calm down enough to try and figure out what to do next. Crystal stepped back over to where her rug was and sank to the floor beside it. If she died, it wasn't going to be from cold *and* an empty stomach—not while she was surrounded by cheeses, vegetables, and fresh fruit. Grabbing an apple, she wiped it off on her sleeve and began to eat.

"I'm calling the police." A man's voice floated inside the cooler from somewhere on the other side of the door. "I'm the owner of this trading post, and I do *not* tolerate shoplifting."

"But I wasn't shoplifting!" Crystal ran to the door and looked out, but the man was gone.

She went back and sat down again, wondering if Junior and Shorty would be able to get her out. But even if they didn't, not all was lost. Wilkinson believed he'd caught a thief. He probably didn't realize she was the owner of the rug he'd stolen. When the police came, she'd show them her rug and then everyone would know the truth.

Suddenly she heard the door click open, and Junior was shoved inside roughly. He tried to reach back for the handle but missed as a big foot caught him in the back and propelled him forward.

Junior crashed into the boxes of apples, bounced off, then fell to his knees as the door was shut again.

"I was so hoping that you'd gotten away!" she said, reaching down and helping him to his feet.

"They must have a security camera somewhere and a monitor in his office. When Mr. Wilkinson returned he went to his office. Then a second later, he came out and shut the door leading to the hall, and I didn't see him for a few minutes after that. When he came back out into the store again, Wilkinson grabbed me and said I was going to join my shoplifting partner. The good news is that he told his son to call the police." He paused then added, "But I guess that's the bad news, too."

"No, it isn't. My rug is right there!" she whispered, grabbing Junior by the arm and squeezing it. "He *did* steal it. He's the thief, and when the police come they can arrest him."

Junior examined the rug, then did his best to turn it around so anyone looking inside the window wouldn't know it had been uncovered. "It's your rug, all right, but I don't think this is going to be as easy as you think. You're going to have to prove ownership."

"Prove that it's mine? But of course it is!"

"I know that, but they say that possession is nine-tenths of the law. He can say he bought it. He may even have a phony bill of sale."

"But he didn't buy it—he *stole* it or, at the very least, bought it hot and knows it or he wouldn't have put it in the cooler," she said. As an idea came to her, she smiled. "My dad has seen my rug. He can verify it's mine."

"I still think you're in for a fight, and the trader can afford a lawyer."

Junior stepped over to the door, then spent several minutes studying the locking mechanism. "I can get us out of here. This type of lock isn't meant to keep people in." He peered at the rubber seals between the locking mechanism and the door frame, then found a big copper staple in one of the cardboard boxes and worked it free.

Using the sharp edge of the staple, Junior cut through one of the plastic straps from a packing case and pulled it loose. He then slid the plastic strap between the door seal and the frame, working it up and down for several minutes. At last there was a faint tinkling sound.

Junior pushed the emergency release knob. This time it moved, and the lock opened with a loud click. "Let's go," he said.

"And leave my rug?" Crystal shook her head. "No way. You go if you want to, I'll understand. But I'm staying right here. The rug's too heavy for us to carry and still escape on foot, and there's no way I'm leaving without it."

"Birdie, the police won't take your side on this. You're just a kid."

"You're the best friend anyone could ever have—which is why you're in this mess now," Crystal said, then looking directly into his eyes added, "but I have to stay, Junior. I may lose the fight, but I've got to tell the police the truth and see this through. But you should go. This is my fight, not yours."

Wordlessly, Junior took a seat beside her. "We'll see this through the same way we started it—together."

"Are you sure? I have a feeling we'll be facing a truckload of trouble."

"We will be," he agreed, then smiled and added, "But Birdie, you're *always* in trouble. That means you have a lot of experience. I'm counting on you to find a way out of it this time, too."

"I'm almost sure that was a compliment," Crystal said, then leaned over to give him a kiss on the cheek.

He turned his head just then and their lips met. Junior wasn't the least bit shy this time, and his kiss was long and delicious. When it finally ended, Crystal's face felt flushed and she could hear her own heart beating. "You're pretty terrific, Junior," she managed to whisper.

Junior smiled, and she thought he might have kissed her again if the door to the cooler hadn't opened just then. Standing there in front of Mr. Wilkinson was a tribal police officer.

Crystal and Junior stood up and went to meet him, but when the officer pulled out his handcuffs, Crystal's knees very nearly buckled. "We aren't thieves, officer. *He* is," she said, gesturing to the trader. "I'm Crystal Manyfeathers. I'm a weaver, and that's my rug," she said, pointing behind her. "It was stolen from my loom two days ago and I've been looking everywhere for it." She explained about the truck and trailer tracks she'd found at her home as well as the reason why she hadn't reported the theft.

Wilkinson's expression grew hard. "The girl's just trying to confuse the issue in hopes that I'll drop the charges, officer. I *bought* that rug."

"Then why are you hiding it in a cooler?" Crystal challenged.

"It's in here, wrapped up, because I thought I saw some moths on it. I was going to kill them with the cold," he answered, looking only at the officer.

"If that were true, you would have used the freezer. The cooler doesn't get cold enough to kill them," she said, then looking at the officer, added, "Without unwrapping the rug I can describe the pattern and the colors in detail. Won't that prove it's mine?"

"You could have sold it to him, then changed your mind," the officer said with a shrug.

"Unfinished?" Crystal countered. "And would I have slipped it off the loom? No weaver would do that."

"But you never filed a police report," the officer

said, shaking his head. "That might have helped substantiate your claim. As it is . . ."

"But I told you why I didn't do that," Crystal said. "And where's his bill of sale? He'd need one for his taxes, right?"

The officer turned to Wilkinson.

"It's around here somewhere, but I'll have to look. Meanwhile, I want these kids arrested."

The officer looked at Crystal and Junior, his expression now more sympathetic. "We can sort this out later. For now I'm going to take you two in. You can present your case in court."

"But I can't leave my rug! He's sure to get rid of it now!"

The officer handcuffed both of them. "I'm sorry, kids. But you need *proof* that that's your rug, not just a description that matches closely."

"Wait—I know." Crystal glared at Mr. Wilkinson, who was playing innocent. "If you look at the rug closely, you'll see that it *doesn't* have a spirit line."

The Navajo officer raised an eyebrow. "Is it finished?"

"Almost. But I never worked in the spirit line," she repeated.

"I don't know what she's trying to pull," Wilkinson said. "The reason that rug has no spirit line is because I bought it off the reservation."

Crystal glared at him then looked back at the police officer. "Then he didn't buy it from me, like he implied, and I shouldn't know what it looks like. I'm telling you the truth! Why can't you believe me?" Crystal tried desperately to think of a way to get through to the officer.

"What about the photo I took, Birdie?" Junior said. "And the tire tracks we preserved?"

"He's right! I can show you the impressions I made of the tires on the thief's truck and trailer, and I have a photo of that rug while it was still on the loom. Surely those . . ." Her voice trailed off as she saw the officer's expression remain skeptical.

"As I said, you can sort this out in front of a judge. Now let's go, kids."

Reluctantly, Junior stepped out into the narrow hall. Crystal followed, taking one last look back at the rolled-up rug beneath the blue tarp still on the floor of the cooler.

Hearing heavy footsteps, Crystal turned her head and saw both Biggins and Shorty jogging down the center aisle of the store toward them.

"Hey, Elroy," the officer greeted them. "The excitement is over here. Come to back me up?"

"Nah, you didn't need *my* help, Uncle Mike," he answered easily. "Dad's expecting you for dinner tonight. You're still coming?"

Crystal's heart started to beat a little slower now, and she smiled. It looked like Biggins would be able to help them turn things around. As she glanced over at Junior, she saw him nod and heard the Good Luck Song he was singing softly.

"I think I know something about what's going on here, Uncle Mike. I had a feeling that there was probably going to be some confusion about the rug Crystal says belongs to her. Why don't you let me carry it out to your squad car for you? You *are* going to take it with you, right? Otherwise you could be helping the thief—whether it's Mr. Wilkinson, or someone who sold it to him. The guilty person could try and change the rug's appearance, or maybe even destroy it to get rid of the evidence. I'm not trying to tell you your business, of course. . . ."

Crystal held her breath as she saw the officer thinking about it, looking back and forth between her and Wilkinson.

For several moments the room was perfectly still. No one spoke, and the silence was absolute, but Biggins was nodding slightly, trying to influence his uncle.

"In the interest of sorting out the truth, I *am* going to take the rug, Mr. Wilkinson," the officer said at last.

"That's preposterous. These two come in here to

steal my merchandise, and now all of a sudden *I'm* the thief?"

"I'm not accusing you of anything, sir—not yet, anyway. But this situation needs to be straightened out *after* all the evidence is in. If the rug is yours, you'll get it back in due time." He gestured to his nephew. "It's inside the cooler, wrapped up in a blue tarp."

Crystal smiled at Biggins and mouthed the words *Thank you.*

Biggins gave her a nod, then went into the cooler to get the rug.

"If you really do have a photo, you'd better have someone bring it down to the station," the officer said.

Crystal looked at Shorty, who nodded and said, "I'm on it. And I'll bring both your dads, too." He glanced over at Junior, giving him a thumbs-up.

Junior and Crystal were led out of the trading post, then helped into the rear seat of the white tribal police car. The rug was carefully loaded into the trunk.

As they got under way, Crystal finally sighed and gave Junior a weak smile. "Dad'll help us."

"My dad will, too—then he'll kill me."

Chapter Fourteen

CRYSTAL SAT beside Junior at a table in a small locked interrogation room at the back of the tribal police station.

"We've been questioned and fingerprinted," Crystal said in a weak voice as she stared at the traces of black gunk still on her fingers. "What's next?"

"Our photos are going to be added to the Navajo Tribal Police mug files?"

"At least their high-school criminal yearbook version." Crystal tried to joke, then stood and began to pace. The walls were blank, and there was a small glass window in the door, but otherwise there was nothing to look at except each other. "*Where* are our dads?"

"Mine's probably considering letting me rot here," he grumbled, standing up and pushing his chair against the table.

Crystal gave him a worried look. "Do you really

think he'll be angry about this? We *had* to find the rug!"

"Well, I don't think he's going to be thrilled about having to bail me out of jail."

"This whole thing has been such an incredible mess. Instead of having my *Kinaaldá*, I could be facing a judge."

"True, and if your ceremony is canceled a second time, it'll probably never happen. They're too hard to arrange. You've really put everything on the line this time, Birdie," Junior said.

"I know what you're saying. And if all this had happened a month ago, maybe I would have run away and left my rug behind the moment you'd opened the cooler door. But things have changed—no, I've changed. Since Mom died I've been running—in more ways than one—from every problem I have. At first I hated myself for not having been there for her when she got sick. I would have given anything to go back and change what happened. Then, as the days went by, not having her around hurt so much, but I didn't know how to make it stop."

She took a deep breath, then after a moment continued. "So I finally told myself that I wasn't a kid anymore and I didn't need her. I left out the spirit line to prove to myself that I wasn't a little girl who still needed her mom's approval—that I was old enough to make my own choices. But you know what? It didn't work. I still missed her, so the truth is that it was all for nothing."

"No, not for nothing, Birdie. You've come a long way in the past few days and learned a lot about yourself. Now the prophecy—"

"What prophecy, and what does it have to do with me?" she asked. Maybe this was the secret they'd been keeping from her.

Junior hesitated for a second, then nodded at last, making the decision to tell her. "The stargazer who attended your birth said that someday you'd be our tribe's greatest weaver and that you'd bring in a new era of classical weaving."

She looked at him in surprise. "Really? Why didn't anyone tell *me*?"

"I heard that your mom had wanted you to have time to develop your skills without feeling pressured by other people's expectations. After she was gone . . . well, you changed, as you just pointed out. And your dad, I think, was afraid that, in your anger, you'd deliberately set out to make sure the prophecy would never come true."

Crystal mulled over what he'd said. "*Now* I understand why my father thought it was so important for me to go through with the *Kinaaldá*. He wanted me to see myself as a Navajo. He must have believed that would make the difference."

"It will. I know you'll be leaving the reservation to go to college, but I'm hoping that what you've discovered about yourself will make you want to return someday."

Crystal nodded, then sat there looking at the floor and silently thinking about what Junior had said. "How long have you known about the prophecy?"

"About six months. I overheard Dad talking to the stargazer." He stared at his shoes then and in a barely audible voice added, "But it didn't come as a surprise to me. I've always thought you're special."

Crystal looked up at him. "You are, too," she whispered.

He started to say something, then turned his head toward the door. "They're coming."

Crystal hadn't heard anything, but knowing Junior, she didn't doubt it for a moment. A second later she heard the sound of a key in the door, and three men walked into the room—a uniformed officer, Mr. Tallman, and Crystal's father.

"Dad!" Crystal threw her arms around him.

"It's all right, daughter," he said, holding her tightly.

"No, it's not," she answered, trying hard not to

cry. "I don't know how to prove to the police that Mr. Wilkinson has my rug."

"I know, that's why I brought your yarns—the ones you dyed yourself. The police can match them to the ones in the rug. The blue, in particular, comes from a process your mother perfected, remember? That's why it's such a distinctive color. The police have located another very skilled weaver, and she's comparing the yarns right now. And their lab will run some tests. I think you'll be able to get your rug back by the time we leave."

Crystal saw Junior and his father standing far apart and noticed the hard look on Mr. Tallman's face. Leaving her father's side, she approached Junior's dad. "Uncle, this was all my fault," she said, coming quickly to Junior's defense. "Your son was only trying to help me find my rug. If you're going to be angry, it should be at me, not him."

Junior gave her a surprised look, then shook his head. "No, I knew what I was doing, Dad. I just never thought we'd both end up here."

Mr. Tallman finally smiled. "You both tried to right a wrong, which deserves some credit, and stuck by each other when things went wrong. That's a true test of friendship." He glanced at Crystal then back at his son. "I'm very proud of you. But if there's ever a next time, come to me first. I may be able to help."

Seeing a tall Navajo officer standing in the doorway, Crystal's dad went out into the hall to speak with him. A moment later he returned.

"Good news. They ran some tests and have proven that the dyed yarns used in the rug perfectly matched the samples I brought from home. And Wilkinson had no records to prove he'd purchased the rug legally."

"Will I get my rug back now?" Crystal asked.

"Yes. Apparently their detectives have had that trading post operator under investigation for several months. A judge issued a search warrant, and other stolen merchandise was discovered in the shop's back rooms and at his home. They already have plenty of other evidence, so in deference to our ways, they'll allow you to take it with you so you can use it in your ceremony."

Crystal smiled at Junior. "I've got to go. I still have hours of work ahead of me before Saturday. Will I see you then?"

He grinned widely. "I wouldn't miss it for the world."

On the way home, Crystal felt closer to her father than she had in many months. "Thanks for everything, Dad. If you hadn't thought of bringing the yarn . . ."

"The skills your mother taught you were what really came to your rescue," he said. "We've tried hard to teach you that Navajo traditions can sustain you no matter what the circumstances. Do you understand that now?"

"Yes," she answered softly. Crystal thought about everything that had happened in the past few days. The simple truth was that her modernist ways, which had resulted in her not leaving a spirit line, had let her down. Yet her friends, her culture, and Navajo traditions had come to her rescue. "Mom always said that it would all come together for me someday, and she was right."

It was already dark when they arrived back home, so Crystal was unable to work on the rug, or even mount it on the loom.

The next morning, right after breakfast, Crystal carried the rug out to her loom. Her father helped her reattach it, then went to take care of the livestock while she began to weave.

Crystal skipped lunch and spent nearly all day adding a spirit line, carefully introducing an additional weft of a lighter color all the way from the center to the border.

The weave was so tight it seemed nearly impossible at first, but by using a needle and being infinitely patient, she finally managed to complete the task.

Finished at last, she stood back and studied her work. She'd thought it perfect before, but without the spirit line it really hadn't been. Now it was.

Crystal took the rug from the loom, removed the twine that had connected it to the dowels at the top and bottom, and tied off end and side edging cords at the corners. Ready for the last step, she buried the rug in clean, washed sand she'd moistened with water from the well.

Hearing voices and laughter coming from inside the house, Crystal put away her weaving tools and hurried back in. Aunt Atlnaba, her mother's oldest sister, had arrived, and was already at the stove, warming up some stew she'd brought for their supper.

"Your *Kinaaldá* is tomorrow and you have to be up before daybreak. You must be starving. Have a bowl of stew, then get to bed early. You need to sleep, niece! You'll have no sleep at all tomorrow," she said, giving her a hug.

Crystal returned the hug. Like Crystal's mother, Aunt Atlnaba always smelled of cornmeal and *piñon*. The memories the sweet scent brought back made a lump form in her throat.

"I've got a surprise for you." Her aunt brought out a package from a huge tote she'd placed on a kitchen chair. "This is for tomorrow."

Crystal unwrapped it quickly and pulled out a beautiful black-and-red rug dress. Rug dresses, woven just as rugs were, required special skills before they could be fashioned into a garment. Without the ability to sew a dress of this kind, or the money to buy one, Crystal had reconciled herself to wearing a blouse and jeans and wrapping herself in her own rug. But the dress her aunt had brought her was perfect. "This is such a wonderful gift! Thanks!"

Atlnaba beamed. "It took me forever to make it." She then brought out a shiny concho belt made up of silver shells threaded on a strand of leather. Last of all came buckskin moccasins designed to wrap around Crystal's lower legs.

"Now you've got everything you need. But are *you* ready, niece?"

Crystal nodded. "I am now." The coming-of-age ceremony was far more than just learning the prayers, or baking a cake, or running. It was about honoring who she was—and those who had come before her. Like the spirit line, it represented an unbroken link from the past to the present. Most important of all, by honoring those traditions, she knew that a part of her mother would live inside her forever.

It was still dark when Crystal woke up to the sound of her aunt's voice. The clock on the nightstand said four-thirty, but she got out of bed immediately, too excited to stay in bed a moment longer. Saturday had finally arrived!

The ceremony would be held in her aunt's ceremonial hogan up in the mountains, and that was a good hour's drive from home.

"Hurry and pack up your dress, niece. You can change out of your everyday clothes once we get to the hogan."

Dressed in jeans and a sweatshirt for now, Crystal ran outside, lantern in hand. The rug should have been buried in sand for at least a day, but this would have to do. She scooped it up and brushed away the sand on top, then shook it out completely. Finally she set it on the ground and studied her workmanship by the glow of the lantern. It was worthy of being taken to the ceremony today. Afterward . . . well, she wouldn't be selling it. She had other plans for it now.

Atlnaba peered out of the kitchen door. "*There*

you are!" Seeing the rug, she smiled. "Your mother would have been so proud of you! After you come back from the race, you can throw that one over your shoulders. It'll be just the right thing. Now hurry!"

The drive to the hogan was even bumpier than she remembered. There were no paved highways on this part of the reservation, just gravel roads—if they were lucky. Many homes were at the end of dirt trails that were impassable during bad weather.

Although the road was bad and their pickup old, Crystal still wished her father would drive just a little bit faster. People wouldn't be arriving for some time yet, but there was a lot to do before then. The hogan would need to be cleaned out, fires built, water collected in barrels would have to be boiled, and a hole dug into the ground. It seemed an almost impossible task for the three of them to finish before the *hataalii* arrived.

"Do you think we'll be able to get everything done on time?" Crystal asked her aunt for the third time since they left home.

"Of course," her aunt assured her once again. "Remember, my husband's family will be coming early and they'll help. But this is *your* ceremony.

It's up to you to make sure that everything goes smoothly."

By the time they arrived, other relatives had cleaned the hogan and started the first fire, and the hole for the ceremonial cake had been dug.

Crystal went inside the hogan with her aunt and changed into her ceremonial clothes. Then, sitting in front of Atlnaba, she waited for her aunt to fix her hair.

"This is it," Atlnaba whispered. "Your ceremony officially begins when I start brushing your hair with the grass brush." As she began, Atlnaba whispered, "The first prayer is the one for Changing Woman. Our family will all sing with you, so don't be nervous."

After her hair had been tied back, the *hataalii,* Mr. Tallman, and about three dozen other people—neighbors, including Junior and his mother, and members of Crystal's clan—came into the hogan. Prayers were sung, then Crystal lay down on the thick mound of blankets placed on the ground. Everyone who'd wanted to share in today's blessings had brought a blanket, and the soft pile was comfortable to lie on.

Then Crystal's molding began. Her aunt kneaded her arms, legs, and stomach, symbolically shaping her into a strong and beautiful woman. When it was over, Crystal stood and, following her aunt's instructions, threw the blankets back to the people who'd brought them. Since it was bad luck not to catch them, no one missed.

Crystal ran like the wind that morning, heading toward the east, where each new day began. Then, as soon as she returned, it was time for her to prepare the cake. Wood was placed in the hole and the fire started, as Crystal prepared the batter and began to mix it with the stirring sticks. It was hard work, but Atlnaba soon joined in and began working alongside her.

"Pace yourself," Atlnaba advised.

By the time all the cornmeal had been mixed, Crystal's arms were weary, but she still had to grind some corn on a grinding stone for the blessing. After more than an hour, it was time to sew the corn husks together. She had to make two sheets of corn husks—one for the top of the batter and one for the bottom—to protect it and keep it from burning. By the time the husk covers were ready, nothing but hot coals lined the hole. After one of the corn-husk sheets was placed over the coals, Crystal poured in the batter, then the second corn-husk cover was placed over the top.

Seconds after she finished, Crystal stepped back and, in one panicked moment, realized that she'd totally forgotten what she was supposed to do next. Her mind had gone completely blank.

"Bless the cake," Atlnaba whispered, handing Crystal the basket of cornmeal she had ground earlier.

Crystal sprinkled it across the cake, moving to the east as she circled it. Then all the guests followed her lead, doing just as she'd done.

Seeing Junior, Crystal smiled, but before she'd even had a moment's rest, Atlnaba came up. "We'll cover it up now, then light a small fire on top. The cake will cook slowly until tomorrow."

Many more tasks followed. Finally, as darkness fell, Navajo Songs filled the air. At first, only the *hataalii* prayed, but soon, one by one, the others in the hogan with them began to chant, as well. Crystal, despite the long ordeal, felt alive and revitalized as the flames leaped and danced, chasing the shadows in the hogan away. Tonight, the Holy People would rain down blessings on all who'd attended.

After a night of sacred prayers in which she had to sit still with her legs stretched out before her and her back straight, her body ached, but Crystal never flinched. As the predawn light brightened the desert floor, Atlnaba nodded at her, and Crystal stood and walked to the door of the hogan. The time had come for her final run. In this race, everyone would chase her. As Crystal stretched in preparation, she saw Junior giving her a thumbs-up.

Crystal took off toward the east with everyone shouting and laughing behind her. She raced for half a mile, then circled and headed back. As she approached the hogan once again, her aunt held out the rug Crystal had crafted. Wrapping it around herself, Crystal went inside and rested until dawn's first light bathed the desert in a soft glow.

No longer a child, but a woman, she went outside to greet everyone. Crystal could see the welcoming acceptance in the eyes of all the women gathered there. She was one of them now.

Later, as Crystal gave everyone who'd attended a piece of cake, Atlnaba came over to stand beside her. "The cake is perfect, niece. We believe that if the batter is still gooey in the morning, then the woman will have a hard life. But yours came out just as it should."

Crystal took the heart of the cake—the center piece—to the *hataalii* and thanked him.

"You've honored our ways and you should be very proud of yourself," Mr. Tallman said. "Do you feel differently now that you've gone through your *Kinaaldá*?"

Crystal smiled wearily and nodded. "I didn't think I would—not after all I've gone through already—but I do. I'm now part of something much bigger, yet I still get to be me."

"All you experienced made you wiser," he noted with a smile.

"Definitely—*much* wiser!" she said with a laugh.

Seeing her father outside, Crystal went to join him. She slid the rug from her shoulders, folded it and held it out to him. "This is for you, Dad."

With a nod he took it from her hands. "I've never been more proud of you, daughter. Your mother would be too."

Crystal hugged him tightly, glad that her family was finally together and in harmony once more.

As her father walked away to say good-bye to some relatives, Junior came up to her.

Crystal beamed him a happy smile. "Although I've never left, I feel as if I've finally come home again." She leaned toward Junior and gave him a quick kiss on the cheek. "If you ever need help for any reason, just holler and I'll be there."

"Balance," he said with an approving nod.

"Thanks for coming," she said, seeing his father was ready to go. "And Junior?" she added before he could leave. "Walk in beauty."